Dark Matter Heart

Nathan Wrann

Dalton Gang Press | West Haven, CT

www.daltongangpress.com

This book is a work of fiction. Names, characters, places and incidents either are products of the author's imagination or are used fictitiously. Any resemblance to actual events or locales or persons, living or dead is entirely coincidental.

Copyright © 2011 Nathan Wrann

All rights reserved. No part of this book may be used or reproduced in any manner whatsoever without written permission except in the case of brief quotations embodied in critical articles or reviews.

For information: e-mail nw@daltongangpress.com

Dark Matter Heart cover title font "TFArrow" provided with permission from http://www.treacyfaces.com

The author would like to thank Jack Ketchum and Joshua Jabcuga for their insight, inspiration and guidance to send me down this path. A vast amount of gratitude is due Helen Austen for her patience and dedication.

ISBN: 1461179513
ISBN-13: 978-1461179511

For Kimberly, who made me do this.

Author's Note*: Gnaural is an opensource programmable auditory binaural-beat generator created by Bret Logan. Binaural beats can induce a "frequency-following response" (FFR) in brainwave activity. For more information, and to download Gnaural please visit: http://gnaural.sourceforge.net*

"Alone-- it is wonderful how little a man can do alone!"
–H.G. Wells

1

Cor hid beneath the olive green army surplus blanket.

Covered like a fugitive on the run, he thought from the backseat of his mother's beat up Honda. A sliver of dull grey light made its way to his eye through a small gap between the edges of the blanket. For five hundred miles, clouds, power lines, streetlights and tree tops had flashed by.

Twenty hours ago his mother Jane took the first shift, driving North for a few hours out of Los Angeles. They swapped at dusk and he took the overnight drive for nine hours. At dawn, they switched again, he laid down across the backseat and she drove the final leg of the journey.

Even with his knees bent and feet on the floor, the backseat was still too short for his lanky frame to comfortably fit. The cramps in his back and legs had disappeared hours ago, replaced with a tingling numbness that plagued him for the last half of the trip. His poor circulation normally made him more susceptible to the pins and needles. A full day's worth of it and he was close to the breaking point.

Cor felt the car roll to a stop and peered through the gap in the blanket. A telephone pole with a half dozen lines and a hazed over streetlight broke up the small bit of solid grey November sky overhead.

Jane reached around from the front seat and tapped the blanket lightly.

"We're here!" His mother said. "It's a beautiful day," she added, positively beaming.

She knew that moving here was a good change for her son. It gave him a chance for a new start, and she was willing to do anything for him. Even if it meant leaving her life behind in sunny Los Angeles and beginning over in the misty Pacific Northwest.

Cor didn't understand what she was so happy about.

He cloaked his head and shoulders with the blanket and sat up to get a better view of the neighborhood.

So this is my new world? The fugitive life begins here, on Drury Street.

Fugitive from what? He thought. He wasn't running from anything and hadn't done anything wrong. Jane had been referring to the move as 'a new beginning' for weeks. Maybe he *was* a fugitive. A fugitive from who he was, from who he had been. The last four years in L.A. were tough. A new beginning here meant an opportunity to be normal. To fit in. To blend in. To disappear. To be invisible.

The small house was uninteresting, indistinguishable from the other houses tightly packed on the block. A small uninteresting front yard and an uninteresting fence on an uninteresting street rounded out the new beginning to help Cor start his uninteresting, unremarkable, unnoticeable normal life. It was perfect.

Jane dangled a set of house keys in front of her son.

"You go on inside. I'm gonna grab some stuff and we can get the rest of it later."

"Okay," Cor said and wrapped his shaking fingers around the keys. He cinched the blanket around his neck with the other hand and stepped out of the car.

At the front door the mist collected on the blanket and rolled down in rivulets of silvery water. It reminded Cor of what was normal. Or rather, what wasn't. A seventeen year old shuffling from the car to the front door, wrapped in a blanket? That wasn't normal.

One minute into my new beginning and normal is already just a dream.

Cor slid the key into the lock. The door swung open. Instantly he knew he was home.

2

The bedroom was almost completely dark. The olive green wool blanket was taped over the only window. Visibility decreased with distance from the light sneaking through the thin gap between the blanket and window pane. A line of grey marked the bare wall where the streetlight's beam ended.

The room was barren. The car only had enough room for a few necessities, food, a few changes of clothes. The moving truck was scheduled to arrive the following day.

Cor lay on his back in the dark on the empty wood floor. His eyes were closed but he didn't sleep.

The Gnaural put him in a good place. His headphone covered ears filled with its steady, droning tone. The tone transformed to a synchronized heartbeat in his mind. It infiltrated him. Invaded his mind and heart. The mental beat generator let his brain shut down for a few hours. Before discovering the program a few years ago Cor's minimal hours of rest were mental chaos. Anxiety. He had no way to rejuvenate. No way to come down.

Cor pulled the headphones from his ears and the beats dissolved into a steady drone in the open air of the empty room, until he hit stop.

Sleep didn't happen for Cor. Post Traumatic Insomnia was what his therapist had called it. Caused by the accident. One of the great side effects of landing face down on pavement after smashing through a windshield and coasting through the air for twenty feet. Four years later Cor had his doubts that the accident was keeping him awake. But if that's what Dr. Dean said, then by God, that's what it was. Cor wasn't going to argue with the doctor.

He raised his hand, partially blocking the line of light streaking down the wall. The light reflected off the back of his pale hand, revealing it. Cor slowly arced his hand out of the light and watched it disappear into the darkness. Then he waved it back into the light, back into existence. Then out of the light where it might as well have never existed. He kept it there, in the darkness, where it belonged. Invisible.

After minutes that felt like seconds Cor got up. The one item that the room's previous occupant left behind was a coat hook screwed into the wall next to the bedroom door. Cor passed through the darkness to the hook, his backpack hung there. He reached into the bag and fished out a drink box. The kind that 3rd graders bring to school with their lunch. He popped the straw off the side and removed the cellophane wrapper as he crossed the room to the window.

The world on the other side of the glass hadn't changed since Cor and his mother had arrived earlier. It was darker but still a small, thin street lined with small thin houses and small old cars parked along the curb on either side. Streetlights and porch lights glowed through a fine mist.

Cor sipped the drink box dry.

Time to see what this new world has to offer.

3

Cor took inventory of the few night denizens populating the diner. It was, for the most part, what he expected to find in this working class neighborhood at one AM on a Tuesday.

The waitress in her forties working a second job pouring a cup of coffee to-go for the cop talking her up at the counter. The college nerd with a table full of newspapers and books. The couple holding hands across the table from each other while they shared a piece of cheesecake.

Cor had followed the lovebirds here from the past-its-prime art house movie theater a few bocks away. That's what he did. Followed people. Watched people. After the accident he couldn't be a doer, so he became a watcher. None of them noticed him.

Not like Los Angeles. Here, wearing his hoodie and jeans, with his pale skin and long hair, he blended in perfectly. After the cop left, the waitress didn't even notice him waiting to order. She went back to reading a dog eared romance novel. Cor didn't mind but he liked to support the local businesses, even if the most he could do was drop five bucks for a cup of coffee. He especially liked supporting businesses that were open twenty-four hours.

He slid across the duct taped vinyl seat and out of the booth.

"Can I have a coffee, please?" Cor asked at the counter a bit too quiet. The waitress, Marlene, according to her name tag, didn't take her eyes off the book.

"Excuse me ma'am," Cor said a bit louder. He only wanted her attention, not everyone else's. Marlene continued to read.

The bell above the glass and faded chrome front door jangled, pulling Marlene away from the pages of heaving bosoms and throbbing manhood. She squeaked, inhaling sharply and let out a startled "Oh!" Surprised to see Cor standing right in front of her at the counter.

"Sorry ma'am," Cor apologized for nothing, "can I get a cup of coffee, please?"

"Oh, sure, sweetie. I apologize. I didn't see you there," She said and turned to pour a cup from the overheated pot of coffee.

"No problem," Cor mumbled. He looked to see who had come in from the dark to join the gallery of patrons.

A man with a full beard and dark glasses, wearing a tattered Seattle Mariners baseball cap, and long, dingy trench coat walked slowly down the row of booths toward the restrooms. The man swung a white cane back and forth in front of him, sliding the red tip lightly across the heavily worn linoleum floor. The blind man kept his head turned toward Cor, like he was staring at him for the whole walk down the aisle.

The man folded his cane and sat in the last booth, facing Cor.

Marlene cleared her throat, interrupting Cor's attempt to spy on the man through his peripheral vision. He took his cup of coffee from the counter and made his way back to the booth. The man's gaze behind the sunglasses seemed to follow him the whole way. It was creepy. He was creepy.

I'm paranoid. Cor reassured himself and flipped through the pages of "The Stranger!" He used the newspaper, like the coffee, as a prop. Common items diverted attention away from him. The lovebirds flirting over the last bit of stale cheesecake on the plate, they were memorable. The guy with a table full of newspapers and books, he was memorable. A catastrophic mess of documentation covered the table leaving no room for his coffee mug. It wasn't a standard diner coffee mug either. Big and stainless steel he must have brought it in with him. He was maybe a year older than Cor, maybe a year younger. No discernible style to his hair or clothes, plain polo, plain jeans, plain glasses. He wasn't an Aberzombie, probably hadn't been to a mall in years. Slightly disheveled but be was clean, not dirty. He'd be completely forgettable if not for the recycle bin that seemed to have exploded on his table. He must have been a regular, Marlene filled his mug without asking, as she passed his table on her way to the creepy guy at the far end.

What are you looking at, Creeper? Cor said to himself. The Creeper seemed to continue staring at Cor even as he placed an order with Marlene. She poured the last bit of coffee from the pot into a cup and headed back toward the kitchen to give the cook the order.

Enough of this bullshit. Cor slid out of the booth and walked toward the restrooms. He became very self-conscious of his stride. Were his steps too long? Was he bouncing with each step? Were his arms swinging unnaturally? Or were they unnaturally stiff? The journey to the restrooms was a study in discomfort as The Creeper's head swiveled keeping Cor lined up with the lenses of the dark glasses on his face.

Cor pushed through the swinging door to the restrooms, his back stiff, certain that The Creeper scrutinized every move he made.

Locking the men's room door behind him, he released the breath that he had unknowingly held for half the distance from the booth to the restroom. The water from the chipped chrome faucet never warmed as Cor filled his hands with it and splashed it on his face. His reflection was barely visible in the dingy, faded mirror.

"No way he's blind, he definitely saw me," Cor said to his hazy reflection

The motor roared like a jet engine but a weak, pathetic puff of air gasped from the hand dryer.

This is gonna take awhile. Cor thought rubbing his hands under the lukewarm breeze.

He emerged from the bathroom to find The Creeper gone. The blind man left behind a full cup of coffee and a newspaper, The L.A. Times.

Weird.

The newspaper was folded open to the Local section and a headline was circled in red marker.

What the hell?

The headline read:

LOCAL TEEN MURDERED

Cor picked the paper up.

Was this a warning? He definitely left it for me.

"Son of a bitch!" Marlene said from behind Cor, holding a plate of scrambled eggs, "That bastard stiffed me."

"What?" Cor replied automatically.

"He took off without paying. 'Scuse me sweetie." Marlene squeezed past Cor to clear the table.

"Sorry ma'am," he apologized.

"If you call me ma'am again I'm gonna charge you double for that coffee," the waitress said waiving the plate of eggs in Cor's face.

"Sorry," he mumbled. He tucked the newspaper under his arm and retreated to his table.

If The Creeper was still playing the blind man act he couldn't have gotten far. Cor dropped a five on the table stuffed the newspaper into his backpack and headed out. The Creeper was a perfect subject for him to follow.

He threw his hood up to cover his head. The mist had turned into a full drizzle. An aluminum skeleton was the only remains of the awning that once covered the door. The cold rain collected on his hoodie but didn't faze him. He felt better now than at any time in the last four years in LA. Cor squinted through the haze of the drizzle for a sign of The Creeper.

Nothing.

"Can ye spare me some?"

The gravel-voiced request from behind Cor was less startling than the assault on his nostrils. He had been so focused on The Creeper that he hadn't even noticed the beggar squeezed against the faded chrome wall of the diner.

"Can ye spare some change?" The homeless man repeated in case Cor didn't hear him the first time.

"What's it for?"

"The shelter. Those goddamn vultures charge, you know."

"Drugs?" Cor asked, expecting a lie in return but digging into his pocket nonetheless.

"No sir!" The beggar responded with an air of offense, "I'm clean and sober. I swear it. The name's Harvey Cassidy, ask around."

"I don't think that'll be necessary."

Harvey Cassidy's hand remained outstretched, never wavering, during the brief encounter. Cor emptied the contents of his pocket, eighty-four cents, into the beggar's hand.

"God bless you son." Harvey grinned and happily accepted the small bit of change.

Cor took another look up and down the street. Still no sign of The Creeper. Time to call it a night. He had plenty of unpacking to do at home before the first day of school began.

He trotted down the four steps of the diner to the cracked and uneven sidewalk. One more glance up the street and then he turned toward to head home, which was only a few blocks away and a couple of streets over.

Cor got about halfway down the block when he turned back for a look at the diner. Most of the neon was either flickering or burnt out, the chrome was tarnished and faded and the windows were hazed over. In its heyday the diner had been pretty flashy. It probably stood out in the neighborhood. But now it blended in with the cracked sidewalks, chipped and faded houses and buildings accompanying it on the street. The diner belonged here, and so did Cor.

Harvey Cassidy popped open a bent and dislocated umbrella, limped down the steps and hobbled his way up the street in the opposite direction. Cor watched him and considered following one more person before ending his night.

4

Cor hated this. Nobody wanted to be the new kid in school, especially him. He hated the attention. Finish eleventh grade, get through the senior year without making waves and get the hell out. That's all he wanted. No awards, no certificates, no trophies, no friends, no attention. Particularly not the attention he was getting from Principal Dupris.

"What about sports?" Principal Dupris asked Cor, or Jane. The question was floated out between them.

Dupris sat in a high-back, cherry trim, presidential style chair. The dark brown of the supple Italian leather matched the deep mahogany of the vast desk in front of him. The bookshelves, wood paneling and the frames around his High School diploma, Undergraduate degree, Masters and PhD documents also matched the desk. Cor thought the office décor seemed more suited to that of a university president than a suburban sprawl high school principal.

He and his mother sat in a pair of uncomfortable, wooden, stiff backed chairs across the desk from Dupris. In elementary school Cor had been taught the difference between the word "principle" and "principal" by remembering that the "principal" wants to be your "PAL". Judging from Dr. Dupris' authoritarian position behind the battleship sized desk and lack of a handshake offer, Cor didn't get the impression that Dupris was interested in being his "pal".

"No sir. No sports," Cor replied. No awards, no trophies, no certificates. That was the goal.

"Are you sure, Cordell? Sports can be a great way to meet new friends," the principal insisted, making it obvious that he didn't bother to read Cor's file prior to the meeting.

"Cor's medical condition prevents him from participating in sports," Jane explained,

"It's right there in the file," Cor indicated the closed folder on Principal Dupris' desk, "and you can call me Cor, not Cordell."

"Oh, of course."

"No gym either, so I'm gonna need the P.E. requirement waived."

"Sure, sure," he said dismissing him, "Mrs. Griffin, maybe we should continue this conversation privately."

"Cor can hear anything you have to say about him. And it's Miss Griffin," Jane said, emphasizing the *Miss*, "I'm not married." Jane's patience was wearing thing.

"Miss Griffin? Is that his father's name?"

"Not that it has anything to do with anything but Cor's father is not in the picture. He has my last name, not his father's." It wasn't the first time Jane had needed to explain it. "You were saying?"

Dr. Dupris shook his head slightly and blinked, having trouble understanding the naming convention. It was an old, childish habit that dated back to his days in grade school. When he didn't understand something he deflected blame toward an imaginary failing of vision. It didn't work on his teachers then, and it wasn't working on Cor's mother now.

"In that case I'm going to be frank with you," he continued without belaboring the name issue, "we are thrilled to have Cor join our student body. His academics are excellent," Dupris cleared his throat for effect, "however, his record does reflect some behavioral problems."

Cor leaned against the hard back of the chair. Of course Dupris had read the disciplinary portion of the file.

Dupris continued, "with his erratic attendance record and your single lifestyle..."

"My lifestyle?" Jane interrupted. The blood began rushing to her face.

"Mr. Dupris..." Cor started.

"Doctor Dupris," The principal corrected.

"Doctor Dupris, I'm just a normal kid. Those problems in that file? They found me. I'm just here to go to school and that's it," Cor jumped in before Jane flew off the handle.

"Well Cordell, Cor, we were really hoping you would be more involved than that. Most colleges won't even look at you without some sort of extracurricular activity. And sometimes a coach can become a father figure. Someone in your situation might respond well to that."

"Okay. I've had about enough of this shit," Jane said, "He may not have had a father in his life but some coach is not going to guide him down the path to righteousness. I work in a hospital, with real doctors, Principal Dupris. I see the trouble these jocks get in, even with their lovely father figures covering their asses so they don't miss a game. That pile of paperwork on your desk doesn't tell you the first thing about my son. I promise you, you will never have a problem from him, and when he graduates in the top five percent of his class, you can personally apologize to him."

"Miss Griffin..."

"And you can kiss my ass. Now who do we need to see to get his schedule so he can get to class?"

5

Before Cor and Miss Griffin left Dupris' inner sanctum, the principal told them that a student named Taylor Jensen would be Cor's guide for the day. He could find Taylor waiting in the general office area. Dupris didn't appreciate parents telling him what to do and had never been spoken to that way in his office. He accepted that Cor wouldn't be playing any sports but something about the boy, maybe the long hair or pale skin, rubbed him the wrong way. He planned to keep an eye on that one.

The harsh, cold, concrete, linoleum and fluorescent lights of the office reception area were a stark contrast to the warm wood of Principal Dupris' inner sanctum. Only one student sat in the waiting area while a few student aides and administrative types busied themselves by making copies and filing paperwork behind the counter.

Cor assumed the boy sitting on the bench with his nose buried in a newspaper was Taylor Jensen. Jane had been up all night working the graveyard shift and was on her last nerve after the meeting with Dupris. Cor assured her he'd be fine and sent her home.

Taylor didn't look like the kind of kid involved in the ubiquitous high school popularity contest, and didn't seem to concern himself much with current hair, clothing or eyeglass styles.

Cor was relieved. He had hoped he wouldn't get a tour guide who spent the day sizing him up to see if he fit their clique. No awards, no certificates. No friends. At first glance Taylor seemed to be a lot like Cor, non-descript and possibly more invisible, however, Cor recognized him immediately. If the pile of newspapers Taylor had been poring over at the diner in the middle of the night hadn't been so conspicuous Cor probably wouldn't have remembered him.

"Taylor?" Cor said after hovering over him for half a minute without acknowledgement.

"Oh!" Taylor jumped, surprised by the intrusion into his world.

Might want to dial down the caffeine. Cor thought.

"Sorry, I'm Cor Griffin."

"Oh, right! I'm Taylor." He hastily folded the newspaper up, making sure to fold it along all the original creases.

"Must be fascinating."

"What? Oh, the newspaper? Yeah. A homeless guy was killed last night."

"Really?"

"Yeah, it's pretty gruesome. The mainstream media doesn't have the whole story yet." Taylor slid the newspaper into his backpack. Cor caught a glimpse of the inside of the bag. It was full of at least a half dozen other dailies, a couple books and a laptop. He must have picked up a few more since Cor saw him at one AM with newspapers spread over the table at the diner. He had thought Taylor was in college based on the workload. Taylor made no indication that he recognized Cor.

Maybe I'm more invisible. Cor thought.

"So, I'm your escort for the day. Er, not escort, but um..." Taylor stumbled over the words, "um, I'm gonna show you around. You know?"

"It's cool. I know what you mean."

"Let me see your schedule."

Cor handed Taylor the piece of paper.

"All A.P. classes. Nice. Me too. We're in the same first period chemistry class. We should get going. We don't want to be any later to Miss Duncan's chemistry class than we need to be. You'll see what I mean." Taylor said. His excitement about getting to class was apparent.

"We can take our time. I hate chem.," Cor informed him as the two of them headed out of the office and into the hallway.

Despite Principal Dupris' attempts to cocoon himself in Ivy League, dark mahogany excess, the rest of the school was pretty standard. White, heavy-duty linoleum tile floors, an accent stripe of the school color blue ran the length of the hall. Cinderblock walls with rows of lockers embedded in them and windows at every possible location, including a two-foot high rectangular window above the lockers on every perimeter wall.

"What? No way," Taylor responded to Cor's disdain for chemistry, "I love it. Chem and bio are the best. If they taught quantum physics here? I might actually consider it heaven. Not really. But science is my life. Science is life. RNA. DNA, seriously, it makes the world go round. Without science there would be nothing." Taylor said, a bit too fast and without breathing.

"Nothing?" Cor said picking up the role of devil's advocate. It had been awhile since he participated in an actual intelligent conversation. "What if that's all make-believe? When you're looking under a microscope how do you know you're looking at what you're looking at? Just because you think you see it, doesn't mean it's really there. What makes your science text book any more real than the Bible?"

"Seriously? Because it is. It's all proven. That's the point of science. To prove things. And to disprove things. Religion is based on faith, without proof. Science is facts." Taylor's excitement level increased as he made his case.

"To prove what? Maybe it's just fiction?"

"Are you really challenging me? Do you know who you're messing with? I'm Taylor Jensen. THE Taylor Jensen."

"Okay?"

"I'm undefeated. When it comes to science fairs, I've never lost one that I entered. If it's real I can prove it or disprove it."

"What if it's something completely new?"

"I'll still prove its existence. The laws of the universe are set, they apply to everything. Turning water to wine goes against that. Finding something new that fits, that's easy."

"I'm just saying, how do you know a molecule is what it is? How do we know any of this is what it is?" Cor indicated the world around them. He was enjoying the banter as they walked down the hall.

"Okay, if this isn't what it is then all bets are off. But if we go with the theory that this is what it is then, wait, are you really questioning scientific knowledge, theory and laws?"

"I'm just messin' with you."

"Oh. Okay."

"Kinda."

"Unbelievable!"

Cor was trying to hide it from Taylor since leaving the office but his health had been deteriorating while walking down the hall. He stopped and leaned against a locker to catch his breath.

"Hey! Are you okay?" Taylor asked

"Yeah, I'm fine," Cor wheezed. It was a lie that he didn't really expect Taylor to believe. His legs barely supported his weight as he leaned against the lockers.

"No you're not. You need the nurse. I'll go get her."

"No!" Cor snapped at Taylor, "I told you, I'm fine. It'll pass. It's nothing. I have allergies."

"This is allergies?" Taylor asked incredulously. "I'm allergic to pollen and cats but it doesn't make me collapse. Do you need an epi-pen or something?"

Cor leaned a shoulder into the lockers for support and pulled a small pill bottle out of his front pocket. His fingers shook as he tried to grasp the top and twist. Finally his thumb pressed the tab and the top popped. He dispensed a small brown capsule into the palm of his hand and tossed it to the back of his throat. Almost instantly he felt a boost of energy return.

"I'm allergic to the sun. It wears me out over time, depending on my exposure," Cor explained, his breathing beginning to return to normal.

"Good thing you moved here. Two hundred and forty overcast days per year. This just doesn't happen to be one of them. It's the cloudiest part of the country. Highest suicide rate in the U.S. too."

Cor didn't bother to inform Taylor that cloud cover wouldn't help him. He had waged and lost those battles with Jane before moving out here. She couldn't be convinced.

"Any other charming facts?" Cor asked slinging his backpack over his shoulder and straightening up.

"Are you okay? Really?"

"Yeah. Let's get to class."

6

Cor felt his legs turn to lead as soon as they walked through the classroom door. They were late and every eye in the room was on him. The whispers started immediately. He followed Taylor to the front of the class where he was introduced to Miss Duncan, a stunning woman with black hair and thick-rimmed glasses. She looked to be only a few years removed from the sorority house but carried the authority of a warden. Taylor's breathing got a little softer and his heartbeat quickened as he presented the new student to her.

Miss Duncan paused her lecture briefly to sign her initials to Cor's schedule, and introduce him to the class. Cor raised a gangly hand in a failed attempt at an innocuous greeting, but hoped the message was more "Stop staring now" rather than "Hi, I want to be your friend." Miss Duncan started her lecture again before he and Taylor made it to the empty lab station at the back of the room.

"Now I get it." Cor whispered to Taylor.

"Get what?" Taylor whispered back.

"Why you like chemistry so much."

"What? Shut up. She's a genius. Don't let her catch you talking."

A few minutes after staring at the backs of his classmates' heads, Cor hoped they had all forgotten about him. He had barely looked at the class during the awkward introduction and wouldn't have been able to pick any of them out of a lineup. Except one. A pretty girl. Blonde, shoulder length hair. Nice looking, not striking like Miss Duncan. It wasn't her looks that drew Cor's attention in those brief moments, but something else. A gravitational pull.

While the other kids in the class sized him up, she seemed embarrassed for him. Not in a patronizing way, but with sympathy. The way she looked at Cor when their eyes met, and his eyes only met with hers during the introduction, didn't suggest the usual self centered thoughts that kids have when meeting someone new: "Do I want to be friends with the new kid" and "What can the new kid do for me?" The pretty blonde was different. Cor felt her concern for his welfare. She knew he wanted to be invisible. When Miss Duncan presented the class to Cor, the pretty blonde shrunk away from the attention, she wanted to be invisible too.

7

The bell signaled the end of second period Spanish class. Cor found Taylor, eyes glued to his phone, waiting for him in the hall.

"Farmville?"

"What?!" Taylor was startled by Cor's interruption, "Uh, no. Oh, I get it. Ha Ha. No, it's the murder."

"Murder?"

"Yeah, the Harvey Cassidy murder. I mentioned it to you this morning."

"Harvey Cassidy?" Cor asked thinking that the name sounded familiar.

"Yeah, the homeless guy that was killed in the park."

"Oh shit."

"Uh yeah, it's pretty sick stuff. It hasn't been released to the media yet but the murderer did some pretty nasty things."

"Do I want to know?" Cor asked, his mind racing.

"Yeah, the cops think it was ritualistic or it might have been a serial killer. But there's more."

The first bell blared, interrupting Taylor's potentially gory detailing of Harvey Cassidy's murder.

"What's your next class?" Taylor asked segueing a little too easily into a much less gruesome conversation.

"A.P. Art history. With Mr. Gifford. Any good?"

"What's the point?" Taylor responded with a mocking huff. Cor suspected he was being goaded into defending art history as payback for the earlier chemistry debate. He took the bait anyway.

"Seriously? You can look at all the molecules you want but unless you walk through a museum you will never truly understand what makes the world go round. Maybe chemistry and biology and quantum physics can explain life but without art is life really worthwhile? Study art if you want to know a real truth. Art is something I can believe in."

"Pssshh. Whatever." Taylor dismissed the argument with a faux ignorant wave.

"After humans had food, and shelter and were able to survive the night in their cave, what did they do? They made art. They didn't look through microscopes."

"Well Mr. Gifford is no Miss..." A hand landed on Taylor's shoulder silencing him mid sentence. Cor and Taylor turned to face a young teacher, maybe twenty six or twenty eight, definitely not over thirty years old. With the right clothes Mr. Gifford might have passed as a student, but the tie and sweater vest made him look older than he probably was. He didn't demand authority like Miss Duncan the chemistry warden, rather, students in his presence gave it to him willingly. Mr. Gifford carried a classic coolness about him.

"That is one hundred percent correct, Mr. Jensen. Miss Duncan is far smarter than I am and I will be happy to tell her you said so." Mr. Gifford said.

"I uh, didn't mean, you know." Taylor stumbled over the cover up.

"No worries Taylor, I know exactly what you mean. Here's a bit of advice," Mr. Gifford leaned in with a heavy whisper, "Miss Duncan doesn't want to talk about atoms and elements in her free time. You know everything there is to know about creating life in a lab. Take my class and learn about what makes life worth creating. In a year and a half, that's what

Miss Duncan will want to talk about. If she's still available." Mr. Gifford punctuated it with a wink and a grin in Cor's direction.

"Oh, Mr. Gifford, it's not like that at all." Taylor protested.

"Sure it isn't," the teacher nodded and then turned to Cor, "You're the new kid," he said.

"Yeah." Cor admitted.

"Mr. Gifford, this is Cor Griffin. He's in your A.P. Art History Class this period." Taylor jumped in to perform his assigned duty.

"William Gifford," he declared, introducing himself, standing up straight and official and extending his hand to shake. "But you can call me Mr. Gifford."

Cor presented him his schedule rather than his hand.

"I'm Cor."

"And you're taking Art History?"

"Yes."

"What's the point?" Mr. Gifford asked with a nod toward Taylor.

The second bell rang.

"Darn! I'm late. Cor, I'll meet you in the cafeteria for lunch?" Taylor shouted over his shoulder as he hopped into a jog.

"Yeah." Cor shouted back. Taylor threw a "Thumbs up" as he jogged down the emptying hall.

No awards, no certificates, no friends. Damn.

"He's a good kid. Damn genius. Come on in and find a seat." With a hand on his shoulder, Mr. Gifford ushered Cor into the classroom.

8

The students in Mr. Gifford's Advanced Placement Art History class looked like they had been teleported directly from Cor's Art History class in Los Angeles. They were mostly self-proclaimed artists who needed the credit for acceptance to the art school of their choice, where they would spend four years and 150,000 dollars of daddy's money in the pursuit of gainful unemployment. Meet the new class, same as the old class.

Hippies and punks made up most of the class with a couple of Goths thrown in for good measure. None of them made an attempt to fit in with the general student population. In their desperate attempts to be unique, they had all failed and become cookie-cutter Hot Topic sales racks.

With one exception. The blonde from Miss Duncan's class was the only normal one in the room. And the only one with an empty seat at her table.

"Cor, there's an empty seat at Caitlyn's table," Mr. Gifford said. Cor made his way around the outside perimeter of the class to her table. He purposely made sure not to walk through the center of the room where all eyes would be on him.

"This semester the class is working on projects in pairs. Unfortunately it looks like you and Caitlyn are stuck together. I hope that's okay." Mr. Gifford informed him as he got to his desk.

"That should be fine," Cor said, a bit too quiet.

"Hi," the blonde said, with a perfect, subtle flip of her smooth, golden blonde hair.

"Hi," he croaked in reply and sat down. The two of them sat in silence. Both of them were very much conscious of each other's presence. Finally, Cor broke the ice.

"I think we have chemistry," he said and immediately regretted the stupidity of the statement. Caitlyn didn't look his way, making him more self conscious than if he had walked across the room naked.

Invisible. No friends. Drop it, she only knows I exist because someone else isn't sitting here.

"I mean together. We have chemistry class together." Cor said in a lame attempt at damage control.

"Yeah, Miss Duncan's class. First period," Caitlyn said, gracious and calm, conversationally, not snippy.

"Yeah," Cor replied, unable to think of something witty, intelligent or worthwhile to say. She had ignored his clumsy opening line without making a scene. For that he was grateful. And had no interest in ruining the do-over she provided.

Mr. Gifford cleared his throat and commanded the room's attention. Cor shrunk on his stool, dreading the inevitable class introduction. The first day couldn't end soon enough.

"Alright everyone, as you all know by now another demented soul has decided to join our ranks and learn about a bunch of crazed and drugged drunkards with paintbrushes. Cor, please stand and introduce yourself."

Oh God no. Shit no. He stood, pushing the stool back with backs of his legs. The metal stool scraped against the concrete floor making an obnoxious screech. All eyes turned to stare at him.

"Um, my name is Cor Griffin. I just moved here from L.A. That's about it." He started to settle back onto the stool.

"Are you a movie star?" One of the hippies called out and then laughed at his own question.

"No," Cor replied standing back up and withholding his follow-up question: *are you a moron?*

"Do you surf?"

"No," Cor replied tersely again. *My skin is paler than a stretched canvas, do I look like I surf?*

"What art are you interested in?" Mr. Gifford asked, bringing the interrogation around toward something relevant to the class. His question had an immediate soothing effect over Cor, calming his nerves. Since entering the room he had felt different. It was the first time all day he hadn't felt sick. Sunlight shined brightly through the classroom windows but his allergies had subsided. He almost felt normal, even with the pressure of the introduction and his nerves rattled from sitting next to Caitlyn.

"Historical, um, art that shows events from history." he responded to Mr. Gifford's question.

"Good thing you're in Art History," one of the Hot Topic Goths called out, followed by a round of laughs from the wannabe rogue's gallery.

"Mostly religious, occult, mythological," Cor continued his response to Mr. Gifford's question ignoring the heckler. Then added "gothic," in the direction of the goth girl for effect.

"What the hell do you know about goth?" She fired back, taking the bait.

"From the looks of things, the same as you, nothing. Which is why I'm here. To learn."

"You don't know me so don't jump to conclusions," she replied, offended by his response.

"You should take your own advice, Wednesday." Cor popped back at her, figuring that the Addams Family reference would probably be lost on this group.

9

The cafeteria, like the rest of the school, was typical. White tile floor, school mascot, a "Fighting Eagle", painted on the walls, plastic molded chairs, long tables, fiberglass trays, terrible food, all standard issue. Cor found Taylor in the hot lunch line.

"I brought today," he told him, "where do you usually sit?"

"Doesn't matter," Taylor replied.

Cor knew that it damn well did matter. He'd eaten in enough school cafeterias and seen enough bad teen movies about high school to know that everybody sat with their friends in their cliques at the same table everyday. Unless you didn't have friends.

"Alright, I'll find a place." Cor spotted an empty, circular table in the far corner. He weaved through the maze of students and chairs toward it.

He leaned on the table to support himself, his weakness returning after the brief respite in Mr. Gifford's classroom. After taking a few breaths in a futile attempt to regain his composure, he dropped his backpack onto one of the molded plastic chairs and began to unzip it.

"You must be the new kid." He heard from over his shoulder. Cor turned to face the voice. A guy wearing a football jersey with the number 12 on it stood eye to eye with him. Number 12 was about Cor's height but heavier, more solid. Healthy. Behind him was a mountain range of flesh and bone standing on six legs wearing football jerseys emblazoned with a 54, 78 and 69.

"You must be the new kid," Number 12 repeated, with a tight-lipped smile.

"Yup. Today is my first day," Cor responded calmly. He noticed they were tense. Defensive. The four of them seemed to be submerging an agitation just under their collective skin. Number 12 tried to hide it but Cor could tell he felt threatened.

He had been in these situations plenty of times in L.A. The subdued aggression wafted from all of them. He must have invaded their territory, the adrenaline and testosterone was palpable as they tried to intimidate him for his offense.

Cor stayed calm. He wasn't scared. Having died once already, there wasn't much on this planet that intimidated him.

"Are you sitting here?" He asked Number 12. Just because he wasn't intimidated didn't mean he wanted to start a scene.

"You thought you could just sit here?" Number 54 blurted out.

Followed up by Number 78, "you must think you're a big man, thinking you can sit here."

"Nope, sorry, didn't realize this table was taken," Cor replied turning back to his backpack to zip it up.

Taylor approached from alongside the football players.

"Cor, there's a table..."

"What's your name?" Number 12 asked Cor, cutting off Taylor.

"Taylor," Taylor responded innocently.

"Not your name Gaylord, his," Number 69 said indicating to Cor. It wasn't the first time Taylor had heard that nickname.

"I'm Cor, and you are?"

"I didn't get that, your name is Dork? That fits. Hey, the new guy's name is Dork," Number 12 announced to his crew. The three meatheads laughed on cue. Cor finished zipping up his backpack.

Number 69 wrapped his massive hand around the little carton of chocolate milk on Taylor's tray.

"Thanks geek," he mumbled.

Cor's hand shot out and grabbed Number 69's.

"Don't touch his food," he snarled, turning this into something that he had hoped it wouldn't.

Number 12 thrust his hand into Cor's crotch and grabbed a hold of his nuts. He dropped to his knees and Number 12 followed him down to that level, taking a seat in the chair. His hand gripped Cor's groin tightly and he leaned in close.

"Brock's a football player. You don't touch football players. And this is my table Dork, you don't sit here. You don't look over here."

"Trace, stop," Taylor pleaded.

The whole altercation was pretty well under the radar until Number 69, A.K.A Brock, swung his massive arm up and knocked Taylor's tray of food fifteen feet into the air. Number 12, A.K.A. Trace, released his grip on Cor and settled back into the chair. His victim stayed down for a few seconds catching his breath and clearing his eyes.

"Anything wrong here?" Mr. Gifford asked.

"No sir. Dor- er, the new guy dropped a quarter or something," Trace explained.

"Taylor? Cor?" Mr. Gifford asked.

"Yeah, Mr. Gifford. Everything is fine." Taylor covered as Cor regained his composure.

"Trace what's going on?" Caitlyn's sweet soft voice broke the cluster of testosterone.

"Nothin' baby, the new guy dropped a quarter." Trace said.

"Okay then." Mr. Gifford accepted the situation and walked away. Cor used the table to help himself up and grabbed his backpack.

"Welcome to Riverdale," Trace said as Cor and Taylor walked away.

The two boys found an empty table across the lunchroom and sat down. The stares from the rest of the students subsided as they returned to eating their macaroni and cheese or turkey sandwiches.

"Sorry about your lunch," Cor apologized, "I managed to save this for you." He handed Taylor the chocolate milk.

"You held onto this?"

"Yeah. They aren't as tough as they look."

"You don't need to apologize. I should have given you the heads up about that table. Are you okay?"

Cor popped a straw into his juice box and took a sip.

"Yeah."

Taylor struggled with the chocolate milk carton. The flap tore back and he tried to scrape open the mouth with his fingernail, pulling at it until it shredded apart, barely looking like an opening to drink out of.

"Oh, hey, Congenital Erythropoeietic Porphyria," Taylor declared examining the mangled milk carton.

"What?" Cor asked. His attention was focused on Caitlyn at the table with the football players. She looked out of place.

"Congenital Erythropoeietic Porphyria. That's what you have, right? Sun allergies? It's what makes you sick?"

"Oh. Yeah."

"I looked it up. It said it's inherited, maybe you got it from your dad."

"Maybe. I think I got it from a blood transfusion. She doesn't seem like the type that would go for a football player."

"She isn't, but whatever Trace Edwards wants, Trace Edwards gets. A blood transfusion?"

"Yeah, I was in an accident. A bad one."

"I know what you're thinking. She's smart, cute, perfect in every way, right? She's my biggest competition for valedictorian next year. Now that she's with Trace she'll also be prom queen and homecoming queen. Not that I think I have a chance at prom queen or homecoming queen. I mean I don't want to be prom queen or homecoming queen. But it's just one more thing she's a lock for. Forget about it. Move on. Trace'll kill you."

"He doesn't scare me." Cor said and took the last sip from his drink box.

10

"I made it through my first day without getting sent down to the Principal's office a single time. My mom is gonna be so proud," Cor said.

"Is that common for you? Getting in trouble?" Taylor asked, swapping books out at his locker and ignoring the joking tone in Cor's voice.

"You saw how it went today. Trouble finds me."

"Yeah. Hey, I gotta run to a tutoring session." Taylor closed his locker and spun the dial.

"Okay, I'll catch you tomorrow then."

"Yeah?" Taylor asked unable to hide the surprise, "Alright, see ya." He jogged off down the hall.

"Hey Taylor!" Cor called after him, "Anything new with that murder?"

"Yeah, it's crazy! I'll fill you in tomorrow." Taylor bounded down the hall and disappeared around the corner, leaving Cor to wonder if his new friend recognized him from the diner last night.

11

Cor shuffled through the nearly empty halls of the school. Despite Taylor's factoid of two hundred and forty overcast days per year, the sun shone brightly outside and he dreaded the walk home. He needed to kill a few hours at the school until the autumn sun hung low enough in the sky.

Wandering the halls he came across an empty interior classroom. It was a music classroom with a piano at the front and no windows. Across the room from where he entered was another open door leading to a parallel hallway. Cor set his backpack down next to the piano and his loose books on top. He pulled the bench out and took a seat. The windowless room gave him a sense of relief. It was a slight reprieve from his illness. Different than the feeling he had in Mr. Gifford's room but still better than how he felt most of the day.

Caitlyn's voice carried into the room. He could hear it coming from the other hallway, opposite the door that he came in through. Leaning back on the bench and straining to look out the doorway he saw her with Trace at a locker across the hall. Cor opened his backpack and pulled his last drink box from the cooler inside. He popped the straw and took a big sip.

Caitlyn and Trace's conversation found its way to his ear and he didn't shut it out. It was mostly typical high school romance talk. He insisted nothing happened at lunch and apologized for his friends making a scene. Her body language said she didn't believe him so he threw on the sad puppy-dog eyes that had worked so well in the past and apologized for being a dumb-ass football player. He said he could never rise to her level and he wasn't worthy of her. She reassured him that he wasn't dumb. He questioned their commitment because they hadn't, *you know,* yet. He put on a sad and humble act. She stroked his ego. They kissed and he ran off to football practice.

Tomorrow would be a new day. He wouldn't be the new kid anymore. He would just be another kid passing time in high school. Cor welcomed the anonymity that awaited him. But at this moment an intelligent, pretty girl stood right outside the empty piano room. He was invisible to her. Unknown, unless he made himself known. For the first time in four years he felt the need to draw attention to himself.

His fingers dropped onto the keys of the piano. The first note was struck. Then the second and third and on into the song. The music flowed from the piano. Following the opening instrumental Cor softly sang the lyrics, just loud enough. It was a slow, soft sweet song about the invisible forces that draw two people together. When he finished the second chorus and struck the last note the sound hung in the air like mist and slowly dissipated. He stared at the keys aware of, but not acknowledging her presence in the doorway.

"That was beautiful," She said with an air of honesty.

"Ohh, thanks." Cor feigned surprise that she had overheard him. His nerves began to rattle as his initial bravado wore off. "It isn't finished yet."

"Did you write that?"

"Yeah. It's called Gravity," He said sheepishly.

"How did you learn to play?"

"I taught myself," he replied. Insomnia had opened up so many more productive hours of the day. Cor closed the key guard and started collecting his books. He could sense she wanted to say something.

"Look," she started, "I don't know if something happened in the cafeteria today. I think something did but Trace isn't really that bad. Deep down he's a good guy."

Cor could tell that Caitlyn wanted so badly to believe that. He didn't want her to make excuses for Trace. He wanted to be mad at her for being with the football player but even at this distance, with half the room between them, he could feel the honest white purity of her heart. She was fully invested in the unfaltering belief that Trace was a worthy project for her. That she could change him and make that deep down good guy a reality. Cor knew that was what made her a good person. That was what made her better than him.

"You can tell a lot about a person's character by the company they keep." He regretted saying it as soon as the words left his mouth.

"He can be pretty sensitive when we're alone."

"I'm sure he is. I won't hold it against you. You seem like a nice person. Maybe I just don't understand." Or maybe he did understand that whatever altruistic sense of duty put her with Trace might also allow her to be with him.

"Maybe," she said letting the word trail off as she looked at her hands or her shoes or the floor, anywhere but at Cor. "I'll see you tomorrow," she added.

"Sure."

She turned to leave but paused, "that really was a nice song you know. I'd like to hear it when it's done."

"Okay,"

Caitlyn smiled and was gone.

Cor finished gathering his books.

12

He was barely through the door of the music room when a massive arm wrapped around his neck. The books and papers in his hands dropped to the floor and scattered across the hall. His hands gripped the forearm to try to pry it free. The attacker lifted him off the ground by his neck and pressed him into the wall of lockers. His massive body leaned against Cor forcing the air from his lungs. He could feel his ribs crack.

"I don't know what you're thinking," his attacker said with hot breath into Cor's ear, "You stay away from her."

The forearm released its steel-trap grip around Cor's neck and he crumpled to the floor gasping.

"You just made your life a living hell, pretty boy."

Cor looked up clutching his throat. Number 69, the one they called Brock, loomed over him. With nothing left to say Brock lumbered down the hall, shoving an on-looker out of his way, just for standing there.

Cor crawled along the hallway collecting his books and catching his breath.

"Rough day?" Mr. Gifford said, seeming to appear out of nowhere.

"I guess. I just tripped."

"Must have stumbled over a Brock," Mr. Gifford quipped back.

"Sure." Cor said, leaning on the lockers to help himself up.

"Want a ride home?" Mr. Gifford offered.

"Nah, I'll walk. My mommy told me to never get in a car with a stranger."

"I'm hardly a stranger, besides walking might not be the best idea." Mr. Gifford indicated to the sun still shining brightly in the cloudless sky.

"What?"

"I know about your allergy. Dr. Dupris briefed us on your situation."

"Ah, my *situation*. Everybody be nice to the sick kid."

"Don't worry about it, your secret is safe with me. Come on, let's go."

13

Cor didn't know what he expected Mr. Gifford to drive, but he sure didn't expect it to be the 1970's era, hippie party, mystery machine, van that they got in. Wall to wall carpeting, a card table that turned into a bed and red velvet curtained windows adorned the vehicle from the Age of Aquarius.

"What else did Principal Dupris tell you about me?" Cor asked as they pulled out of the school parking lot.

"He told us you got in a lot of trouble at your previous school."

"I wouldn't say I got in a lot of trouble. I got in a little bit of trouble a lot of times. Let the record reflect that it was never my fault."

"Of course not. Like with Brock, right?"

Cor turned to look out the side window, annoyed that Mr. Gifford didn't believe him.

"Yeah, just like that. I'd prefer to pass through unnoticed. Never be seen."

"The invisible man, huh?"

"Yeah. What else did Dupris say?"

"He said you didn't have a father. He made sure to point that out." Mr. Gifford said matter-of-factly. Cor couldn't remember a time that a teacher had told him about a conversation he'd had behind closed doors with the principal.

"Damn. Now he's let all of my secrets out," Cor said flatly, "yes, it's true. Immaculate conception exists. I am the second coming of Christ. I have no father."

"Well that explains the hair." Mr. Gifford said with a smirk.

"Oh, you don't like? I thought it fit perfectly with the aesthetic you've got going on in this ride. Next time I'll be sure to accessorize with my tie-dye and Birkenstocks."

"To each his own, man," Mr. Gifford drawled with a High-Times affectation.

"Yeah, fatherless. That's me. You know, it's not like I don't have a father. I do have one, he's just a spineless, gutless coward. I've never seen him. Never once. What kind of man abandons his responsibility like that? He took off when my mother told him she was pregnant. She made sure to sack me with his name though." Cor paused and looked out the window. "And all this father figure crap from Dupris? *A coach can be a father figure.* Fuck you! Have you seen how the football team behaves? In all honesty I have a father figure. No man could ever teach me more about owning up to responsibility than my old man has. Best lesson I've ever learned. I know what it's like to be abandoned. I know what it's like to be on the receiving end of that. And I know I would never treat someone the way he's treated me."

Cor wiped his sleeve across his eyes. He stared out the window in silence the last few blocks to his house.

"Thanks for the ride," he said as Gifford pulled up in front of his house.

"Anytime. By the way, Taylor's a good kid. If you're looking for a friend you could do a lot worse. His friendship will pay dividends to you. Trust me."

"Sure."

No friends. Stay invisible.

The van disappeared down the road leaving Cor behind thinking Mr. Gifford might be one of the good guys.

14

Ten o'clock pm, the same time every night. Cor's eyes opened. The rhythm of the Gnaural broke as he pulled the headphones from his ears and dropped them on the mattress. He felt good, refreshed, rested. Strong.

He spread the curtains, lifted the blinds and raised the shade covering his bedroom window. The grey light from the full moon filled the room. The sky was still as clear as it had been during the day.

The moving company had delivered the boxes and furniture earlier in the day. Cor hadn't bothered to unpack anything except for his keyboard. After he played his song for Caitlyn, inspiration had struck and he had worked for a few hours on it before resting. The rest of his stuff cluttered the floor in plain brown cardboard boxes labeled with black magic marker.

Cor got dressed in his nighttime uniform, which was the same as his daytime uniform: plain t-shirt, plain hoodie, plain jeans, chucks. Nothing that stood out.

The normal routine would have been to wake up Jane but she was already making noise in the kitchen, so Cor headed down the hall.

"Hi," he greeted her and grabbed a drink box from the refrigerator. Jane's cup of coffee smelled delicious.

"How was your first day?" She asked.

"The usual," Cor mumbled, dreading the interrogation.

"Cor, it can't be the usual. Not again. You have a chance here to start over."

"You're right, but there's nothing I can do about it." Cor sucked on the straw.

"You can stay out of it. Don't get involved. Keep your head down and just graduate next year, that's all I ask."

Yeah, be the invisible man, tried that. "And then what?"

A car horn sounded from in front of the house.

"That's my ride," Jane said.

"Your ride?" Cor asked disappointed that Jane was just saved from the difficult part of the conversation where they talk about his lack of a future.

"Yeah, another nurse lives a few blocks away. We're carpooling. See, a new start. Stay out of trouble tonight." She kissed him on the forehead, grabbed her bag and darted out the front door.

Cor went into the living room and peeked through the gap between the shade and the windowsill of the front window. A blonde guy sat behind the wheel of a Honda parked in front of their house.

15

Stay out of trouble. Shouldn't be hard, Cor thought. Trouble only found him at school. The people that came out after dark must be more tolerant. Or scared.

The diner was the first stop on his agenda. He was curious to see if Taylor was moonlighting again, his face plastered to the newspapers. Maybe he'd be ready to spill his exclusive info about the Harvey Cassidy murder.

Cor's plans changed when he was a couple blocks away from the diner. The Creeper was standing on the front steps of the faded chrome and flickering neon beacon. The strange man had apparently been waiting for Cor. He popped the collar up on his grimy coat and began walking up the street, away from Cor. The cane was gone but the dark glasses and hat were still part of the costume. Cor pulled his hood down low over his eyes and discretely picked up the pace to try to catch up.

The Creeper rounded a corner up ahead so Cor broke into a jog to catch up. Just as he turned the corner, The Creeper vanished down another side street. He was still a few blocks away. Cor hadn't closed any distance on his target.

He sprinted to the intersection to avoid losing The Creeper. He needn't have bothered though, his prey was waiting, still a few blocks away, at the entrance of a wooded park. When Cor got to the corner his target slipped past a decorative wrought iron gate and disappeared into the opaque darkness. A wall of high, thick bushes surrounded the perimeter of the park and the interior was pitch black due to the thick overhead canopy of foliage. The only way in was past the wrought iron gate. Cor bolted across the street to follow The Creeper.

The park was a thickly wooded suburban forest. Asphalt walking paths wound between the trees. Occasional park benches dotted the pathways at random intervals. The moonlight barely broke through the dense leaves overhead. A few sparse decorative lampposts did little to illuminate the park. The Creeper was nowhere to be seen. Cor had lost him.

A strand of yellow police crime scene tape flapped and whipped in the breeze tied to the armrest of a park bench. It was the only evidence that this had been a crime scene earlier today. And before that, it had been Harvey's bench.

"Should have gone to the shelter like you said you were going to," Cor quietly gave the dead man advice that was too late to receive.

The Creeper led him here on purpose, he was sure of it.

What does he know about me?

Standing at an old crime scene in the dark wasn't going to give him the answers. He turned to head back toward the park entrance and stepped right into the path of a midnight jogger. The runner slammed into Cor. The impact sent the runner sprawling across the ground.

"Whoa! Are you alright?" Cor asked, stepping toward the runner and offering to give him a hand up.

"Watch where you're going," the runner shot back, helping himself up and brushing off. He immediately broke back into a jog and Cor watched him wind his way down the path between the trees and disappear into the darkness.

"Me? You better watch where you're going. It's dangerous out there tonight." Once again Cor found himself delivering advice that was too late to be received.

16

Cor knew he would hear about it from Jane if he didn't at least do a little unpacking. After leaving the park he had time to kill before school started. He spent the morning in the kitchen putting away dishes, silverware, pots, pans and other utensils that were never used. With every box he opened he asked himself the same question: *Why do we have all these dishes?*

The first thing he unpacked was the small kitchen television. It fit perfectly on the counter and the local early morning newscast kept Cor company while he found places to put cheese graters, shish-kebob skewers and apple corers. Anchorman Tom West, with his graying soft crew cut, square jaw and bizarrely hip glasses along with the rest of the goofball morning crew filled the small screen with their light banter, weather reports and traffic updates.

The "Breaking News" graphic swooped across the screen accompanied by dramatic music and sound effects grabbing Cor's attention. Tom West stared out of the screen with his serious face on and glasses off.

"Donna Hale is live at Odel Park where a grisly discovery was made early this morning."

Cor put the stack of plates down on the counter. Donna received his full attention. The wrought iron gate and high bushes of Odel Park filled the background behind her.

"Good morning Tom, good morning everyone," Donna said into her microphone, "early this morning a jogger's body was discovered by an elderly couple on their morning walk through Odel Park. Police have identified the victim as Steven Tomlinson, 32 years old of East Riverdale." Donna Hale's image was replaced on screen by a snapshot of a man enjoying a sunny day on a sailboat. The on-screen graphic identified him as Steven Tomlinson. Cor recognized him as the jogger from the night before.

Donna continued her report: "The police department hasn't provided us with any information or details about the nature of the death and has refused to speculate on whether this is connected to the homeless man that was found here yesterday. Many of the officers, detectives and EMTs returning from the scene have been very shaken up by the state of the victim's body. Most of them were speechless and the only ones willing to talk haven't said anything other than robbery does not appear to be a motive. We'll have more throughout the day on this disturbing breaking story. Tom, back to you."

17

Taylor sat on the front steps of the school while hordes of students brushed past him on their way to class. His attention was firmly focused on the newspaper in his hands and he didn't notice Cor standing in front of him, wheezing from climbing the dozen steps or so. Despite the long sleeves, pants and hood, the morning sun was already taking its toll on him.

"Hey," Cor gasped to get Taylor's attention.

"Oh! Hey!" he snapped, startled again.

"Any details on that jogger?" Cor was pretty sure he knew which story had captured Taylor's attention.

"A couple on-line articles. Nothing in the paper yet, it happened too recently and the cops aren't releasing anything publicly. I think it's connected to the one from the other night."

"One from the other night?" Cor asked, playing dumb.

"The homeless guy that was murdered." Taylor opened his backpack and selected one of the dozen or so newspapers stuffed in the bag, He smirked when he noticed Cor's curiosity at the newspaper obsession.

"I'm a bit of a news junky," Taylor said, stating the obvious.

"Can't you just use the internet?"

"I do, but I have my reasons."

Cor didn't doubt that. Taylor opened the paper up and folded back three or four pages. He handed it to Cor.

"Here, read."

"The body of a homeless man, identified as Harvey Cassidy, was discovered in Odel Park early this morning, etcetera etcetera," Cor read from the paper, "Yeah? You mentioned this yesterday. What makes you think they're connected?"

"Same place. Same time. What's missing from that article? Cause of death. Details. The police didn't release anything. You know why? Because there are very specific things about this murder and they knew that the killer would strike again. They won't release the details because they don't want a copycat and they want to weed out the false confession nut jobs." Taylor lowered his voice as if the kids running by to class cared about their conversation. "Nobody is supposed to know this but both of them..."

"Had their carotid arteries slit and all of their blood drained?" Cor finished Taylor's sentence.

"Yeah. How'd you know?" He asked with shock and a twinge of disappointment that he couldn't surprise Cor with his inside info.

"Let's call it déjà vu. If the police haven't released any info, how do you know?"

"I'm going into forensic science. I do a freelance internship down at the crime lab. You know what? There's something else. I was going to tell you this yesterday about the homeless guy. At that point it was just sick. Now it's weird."

"What?"

"They both had words carved into their flesh after their blood was drained."

"No shit?"

"Yeah. Harvey Cassidy had *Not clean. Not Sober* carved into his chest and the jogger had *Watch where you're going* sliced into his back."

"Jesus."

"Yeah, freaky."

"What are you doing after school today?" Cor asked him.

"Nothing after my tutoring session, why?"

"You wanna be a detective? Meet me in the library at four o'clock. And in your free period check as many back issues of the L.A. Times as you can. Start with last week's paper and go back five years. Local news. Inside pages. Never the front page."

"What am I looking for?"

"Déjà vu."

18

Mr. Gifford rattled on and on with his lecture. Cor didn't mind, his allergy seemed to take a break during Art History and he was sitting mere inches from Caitlyn. He felt a bit awkward seeing her today. When she arrived to class a little late she marched straight to the table, avoided eye contact with Cor and barely whispered *hi*. In chemistry she never acknowledged that he was in the room. Cor was sure that word of Brock's assault on him had spread. She had probably heard about it last night or early this morning. He figured she was trying to protect him or she was embarrassed by the whole situation. Or maybe she had broken up with Trace and was nervously waiting for Cor to ask her out.

The anxiety began to settle in. Maybe he had done something wrong. Did he say the wrong thing to someone? Doubtful, he had only spoken to Taylor; he was invisible to the rest of the school. Even as his classmates talked about Brock beating the new kid up, none of them seemed to know it was him. Cor was sure he'd screwed up somewhere. He had messed up and blew any chance that he had with her. She wouldn't even look at him.

The bell rang, interrupting Cor's despair and cutting off Mr. Gifford's lecture. Cor was ready to disappear anonymously into the hall. Maybe Jane would be willing to move again.

"Before you go, I apologize that you didn't get a chance to work with your partners today. You'll definitely get time tomorrow. Cor, Caitlyn, do you have a minute to talk?" Mr. Gifford said, wrapping things up.

Cor's anxiety continued to build. Maybe she was late because she told Mr. Gifford that he made her uncomfortable. Maybe she didn't want to be his partner anymore. Chances are, he'd get stuck with the Hot Topic Goth girl.

"Have you selected a specific focus for your project yet?" Mr. Gifford asked the two students.

"What?" Cor replied, caught off guard.

"We haven't really had a chance to talk about it yet, Mr. Gifford." Caitlyn answered.

"Do you have anything in mind, Cor?" Mr. Gifford asked.

"Um, I thought maybe researching the validity of myths through historical works of art might be cool."

"The validity of myths?" The teacher questioned.

"Yeah, like, historically speaking, are vampires real? For example, can depictions in artwork show us evidence of that?"

"Vampires? Like Snooki and Edward?" Mr. Gifford said. Cor couldn't tell if he was joking.

"Well, kind of. I'm not really interested in the new popular ones. Those are just fictitious bastardizations based off the pop culture myths that have been recycled since Dracula. What I'm interested in is comparing historic, standalone works with some modern day, real evidence. Maybe. It's just a thought. Caitlyn might not even want to do it."

"It isn't unicorns and Pegasus but it could be interesting. I'm up for it," she said, more chipper than Cor thought she would be.

"Great!" Mr. Gifford chimed in, "I was worried you two might be a little behind the class since you got a late start."

"I have to go, Trace is waiting for me." Caitlyn declared, killing Cor's theory that she had dumped the meathead. She grabbed her books and dashed out the door. Cor chased after her into the hall.

"Caitlyn wait!" He called ahead. She stopped and turned. "Can I get your number?" He asked.

"What?"

"Can I get your number? So I can call you for the project?"

"Oh, yeah, of course." She pulled a pen from her bag and grabbed his hand. Cor tensed when their skin touched.

"You're freezing," she blurted out.

"Yeah, bad circulation. I got in an accident as a kid. Long story."

The first bell rang. The hall emptied as kids ran by to get to class. The warmth of Caitlyn's hand transferred to Cor's. She put the pen to his palm and wrote her number. Her hand lingered for a moment, holding his, unable to let it go. She stroked her thumb across the meat of his palm. She lifted her eyes and they met his.

A student rushed by, bumping into her, springing her from the moment. Caitlyn released Cor's hand and silently turned. She walked away without a word.

Cor glanced through the windows to the courtyard. Brock and one of his other mountainous friends sat on a picnic table. Their eyes focused on him. Cor grinned and shot a wink in their direction. He couldn't help himself.

19

At four o'clock Cor found Taylor in a far corner of the library. He was chest deep in newspapers stacked on a table. Cor dropped his backpack on a chair and leaned on the table exhausted.

"How long have you been here?" Cor asked.

"Since second period. This is crazy." Taylor answered without lifting his eyes from the paper he was reading.

"What about your classes?"

"I told them I needed to conduct research. I'm the least of their problems." Taylor set the newspaper down and took a sip of his large coffee. Cor noticed it was the same mug he had at the diner. Finally, he exhaled deeply and looked Cor dead in the eye.

"There are countless murders in these newspapers. Yet three or four times a month there's a murder that is a dead ringer for the homeless guy or the jogger. No details. Always described as disturbing and sometimes it's described as a stabbing or slashing. It's all very circumstantial though. Do I believe because I want to?"

"Is that for all five years?"

"No. The first year there was nothing, then, like clockwork."

"Exactly. Where are the papers from last year?"

Taylor pushed a stack of L.A. Times toward Cor. He had them all open and folded to the stories that resembled the two recent murders.

"I'm not familiar with L.A. but I started tagging the locations in Google Maps and last year they were all pretty close together." Taylor said.

"Yup, I agree."

"And no specific details released by the police. Not even in follow up stories."

"Yup."

"And after the final L.A. Murder last week, we look at yesterday's local paper and today's afternoon edition and we find our homeless man and our jogger."

Cor took the local papers and put them in the same stack as the L.A. newspapers from the past year.

"Do the police know about the L.A. murders?" Cor asked him.

"I don't think so. They just think the two Odel Park ones are connected. That the killer is home grown."

"Right. The L.A.P.D. doesn't want to confirm that they have or had a serial killer so they kept some of the details out of the databases. A serial killer would send up flags and the FBI would get involved bringing a whole bunch of red tape and paperwork. There's a big difference between random throat stabbings and a guy that drains the blood from his victims. The L.A. guy was a drainer too."

"How do you know?"

"My mother is a nurse. She works nights. Sometimes the bodies would end up at the hospital before the cops collected them for evidence. Sometimes the EMTs would talk,"

"You have to tell the police about this connection," Taylor said, "you'll be a hero." Cor was afraid he would jump to that conclusion.

"I can't," Cor told him. He hoped but didn't expect those words to put an end to that line of thought.

"Why not?"

"I lived in L.A. while these murders were happening and I live here now."

"You couldn't possibly be a suspect."

"Look, I can't go to the police, let's just leave it at that."

"Then I'll go. This could help solve the case."

"Taylor, nobody is going to the police with this information. The L.A.P.D. couldn't solve these crimes; the cops here aren't going to catch this guy. They don't know what to look for."

"To be honest Cor, I'm not fully convinced that these are all connected. Could be a copycat. Someone that reads the L.A. newspapers or has inside info."

"Damnit Taylor, it's not a copycat," Cor snapped at him.

"How can you be so sure?"

Cor grabbed one of last year's papers from the pile.

"Convenience store clerk, throat slashed. I bought a magazine from him the day of his murder. He gave me back the wrong change and refused to reimburse me." He dropped that paper on the table and grabbed another, "bus driver, I rode his bus." He grabbed the next one, "barista at the coffee shop I went to." He picked up another, "a kid at school, didn't like me." Cor threw that newspaper down, "Get it? I interacted with all of them. I had contact with all of them." He grabs the local newspaper, "Harvey Cassidy, homeless guy. I gave him eighty-four cents the night he was murdered, check the evidence log. I guarantee it was still in his pocket. You know what he told me? He said he was *clean and sober*! The jogger? I ran into him in the park. Right next to Harvey's crime scene bench. Guess what he told me. Go ahead, guess."

Taylor hesitated.

"Go ahead, take a guess."

"*Watch where you're going*?" Taylor whispered.

"That's right."

A heavy silence hung in the air, broken only by Cor's labored breathing and wheezing.

"You didn't. Did you?" Taylor asked. Cor didn't need him to finish his thought to know where he was going with it.

"If you think I did this..." Cor swiped his hands through the newspapers stacked on the table sending them off the table and scattering across the floor. "...then why are you still here? Here's a bit of advice, don't accuse someone of being a serial killer when you're alone in the library with them." He dropped into the chair, too weak to stand.

"Look at you. You're probably the only kid in this school whose ass I can kick. You're a nice kid. Whoever did this isn't right. Why would you show me all this? And besides, Gifford said you're a good guy and your friendship would, quote, pay dividends. Whatever that means."

"What did he say?" Cor asked even though he had heard every word clearly.

"It doesn't matter," Taylor continued, "did you tell him about all this?"

"No." Cor could barely utter the word. He pulled out his pill bottle and tossed a capsule down his throat.

"You think the police can't solve these?"

"Taylor, I promise you, I did not kill these people, but I might be the only one able to catch the guy that did. If I go to the police nobody will believe me. They'll probably arrest me. If I'm arrested I can't catch the killer. When I catch him, you get the credit. That's a hell of a way to start a forensic science career."

"How? Why?" He asked. Cor knew Taylor's interest was piqued. He just needed to sink the hook.

"I thought it was all a coincidence. For a year I was somehow connected to these murders. Like six degrees of Kevin Bacon, except that it was just one degree of me. Then I move here. Two days, two murders. The night Harvey was killed I was at the 24 Hour Diner a couple blocks from Odel Park. You know the one."

"Yeah."

"Yeah, you were there that night too, but I didn't know you then. Someone else was there as well and he left this." Cor pulled The Creeper's newspaper out of his backpack with the circled headline. "He left it for me to find. That local teen in the article worked for the moving company that packed up my house."

"I don't remember seeing you at the diner."

"Not surprising. Most people don't know I exist until I impact them somehow. That's the way I like it. Besides you had your nose stuck in a bunch of books and papers."

"Who left this?"

"I don't know who left it. I call him The Creeper. He looks like a weirdo with a beard, hat and dark glasses. And he had a white cane, like he was blind. It's like he was wearing a disguise. Or homeless."

"He's blind? A blind guy is killing people?"

"No. He was pretending to be blind."

The librarian intruded on their corner of the library.

"Boys, it's almost time to close," she said with a wink toward Taylor.

"Yes ma'am." Taylor politely responded. Her smile further revealed her crush on the boy genius.

"Come on. Let's go to my house. I have a theory. You're going to think it's crazy but I'll tell you about it on the way. I need your help."

"Okay. But who's going to clean up this mess?"

20

During the walk to Cor's house Taylor was bursting with anticipation. He was sure Cor didn't have the solution but if his friend's theory was something truly outside-the-box it could start an excellent brainstorming session. That could result in something to bring to the police. Like Cor said, it would be a great way to kick off his career. Cor could feel the nervous, excited energy coming from him. He hoped that revealing the L.A. murders bought enough respect that Taylor would, at least, consider listening to his theory from beginning to end. Taylor was impatient and skittish the entire walk but had agreed to wait until they got to Cor's house so that the theory could be illustrated with some materials that Cor had.

It was around the halfway mark, past the point of no return, when the anticipation got the best of Taylor.

"So what is it? What's your theory?" He asked Cor, wiping sweat from his forehead and shifting the weight of his loaded backpack. Despite the cool November air, the sun was hanging low and warmed the back of his neck. Cor had his hood up and hands stuffed in his pockets to minimize his exposure. He began to think that Taylor wasn't used to this much walking.

"You want it straight?" Cor whispered, barely more than a wheeze as he labored to put one foot in front of the other.

"Yeah," Taylor answered excitedly. Cor figured that Taylor might be concerned they wouldn't make it to his house. That Cor would drop dead on the spot, overcome by his illness, and then his case-solving theory would die with him,

"How much do you know about vampires?" Cor said, opening a can of worms. Taylor froze in his tracks. A dead stop where he stood. He gawked at Cor, who continued plodding forward.

"Are you freakin' serious? Your theory is vampires? If the police learned the information that you gave me today, and it's not really secret info, you know, but if they discovered it you would be arrested as a major suspect. Or at least a person of interest. And that's all you've got? That's... That theory? That's... I don't even know what that is. It's just stupid. What are you talking about? Like freaked out goth wannabe vampire kids that file their teeth and worship Satan? Yeah. Maybe." The words shot from his mouth like machine gun fire.

Cor had a feeling it would be a tough sell. He hoped that maybe Taylor's science-oriented mind would embrace the unknown to try to make it known. After Taylor's reaction he thought that the existence of vampires might not be considered a legitimate scientific problem.

Cor stopped walking and turned to face Taylor. The low hanging sun shone in his face so he pulled his hood down slightly to shade his eyes.

"No, like real vampires. I know it sounds crazy but hear me out..."

"Cor," Taylor cut him off, "get real. He's just a psycho serial killer. That's it. Vampires do not exist. Maybe he saw 'Near Dark' too many times. If he was a fan of 'Lost Boys' he would have jumped from a train trestle long ago and we wouldn't even be worrying about this. You should probably just tell the police about the L.A. murders. Come forward, it's your best bet."

"I have proof."

"Oh, is Dracula living in your basement? It's impossible to have proof of something that is make-believe."

"What if it's no more make-believe than something like dark matter? There's plenty of research going on for that. Aren't you a scientist? Isn't your life supposed to be dedicated to understanding things that otherwise can't be understood? Didn't people believe the sun revolved around the Earth until a scientist proved otherwise? The only difference here is that when you have the proof, you can't go public."

Taylor looked at the ground and shook his head. He couldn't believe it had all devolved into this. Cor felt badly, Taylor had faith in him and now he had let him down.

"Dark matter is inferred to exist because of the way that known, visible objects are influenced by something that is unknown. A gravitational pull from something that can't be seen," Taylor said, still staring at the ground.

"Known visible objects? Okay. The jogger and Harvey Cassidy. Influence? Blood drained. Dead. Can't we at least theorize or hypothesize that it's the work of a vampire? Humor me. Come to my house and I'll show you. What else are you doing tonight?"

"I'm not going to your house. I'm going to the police."

"Taylor, just give me one..."

Cor halted mid-sentence. A bright blue jacked up 4x4 pickup truck came screaming around the corner. The truck hopped the curb and skidded to a stop on the sidewalk in front of Cor and Taylor. The dark-tinted driver's window rolled down. Brock's grinning; meathead face stared right at Cor.

"Must be my lucky day," the football player grunted.

Cor turned to Taylor, "Run! Get out of here. Go to my house, 42 Drury Street, 6 blocks that way, and wait for me.

Don't tell my mother, don't call the police," he urged him in his most intimidating growl.

"But..." Taylor protested.

"Get the fuck out of here! It's me they want! Go!"

"I'm not leaving you," Taylor insisted. He dropped his backpack on the sidewalk unwilling to abandon his only friend.

"Goddamnit Taylor."

Brock opened his door and stepped out. The other man-mountain from the courtyard, Number 78, got out of the passenger side. Both of them lumbered toward Cor and Taylor.

"You want a runnin' start, pretty boy?" Brock offered Cor.

"I'm not that fast," Cor refused.

"Too bad, it would have been more fun to chase you down. Hear you scream like a bitch when I tackle you on the pavement. Hear that fear in your voice as you struggle."

Cor stepped forward to put himself between the two football players and Taylor. He hoped Taylor would be too scared to get involved and the jocks would leave him out of it.

"I'm not afraid of you. You can't do anything to me that hasn't already been done."

"We'll see about that," Brock grunted with a grin. He pounded his fist into his palm, just like in the movies, as he marched toward Cor. "Next time, you better think twice before getting a girl's number."

Taylor pushed past Cor and stepped up to Brock, "look Brock, he didn't do..."

Brock shoved Taylor over to Number 78, "Shut up Gaylord."

Cor was weakened by the sun, but stood his ground the best he could. He tried to stand tall but slouched over. Brock looked to be a foot taller and at least double Cor's weight. The big man put his palm on Cor's chest and drew the fabric of his hoodie into his fist. Cor's hands hung limp and open at his sides. He made no attempt to defend himself. No attempt to resist.

Brock cocked his arm back slowly. Cor imagined the sound of gears clanking and industrial elastics stretching as Brock's fist pulled back near his ear. The thought of it made Cor smirk a bit.

"Brock!" Taylor screamed and struggled against Number 78's hold. The football player hoisted Taylor into the air. He carried him over his shoulder and body slammed him over the white picket fence into the front yard of the house they were in front of. Taylor hit the ground flat on his back with a solid thud. The wind rushed out of his lungs. Taylor wheezed and gasped unable to catch his breath.

"We told you to stay away from her." Brock punctuated his statement by slamming his fist into Cor's face. The impact of the blow buckled his legs. Brock held his victim up by his grip on the hoodie. Blood streamed down Cor's face through a gash in his left cheek, right below his eye. Cor could feel a throbbing pain from his shattered orbital bone and he lost vision in that eye.

Immediately Brock cocked his arm back again and drove it into Cor's face again. The hit severely dislocated his jaw and the third punch cracked it down the middle. The left side hung slack a half inch lower than the right. Brock released his grip on the hoodie. Cor dropped to the concrete sidewalk like a discarded doll.

"Jesus! Did you kill him?" Number 78 asked, less worried about Cor's well-being and more annoyed that he didn't get some shots in.

Taylor gasped for breath on the other side of the fence. His face contorted with anguish for his friend lying on the sidewalk with a mangled face. Cor glanced over at him and saw his concern. *He's a good kid,* he thought.

Cor didn't want Number 78 to feel left out so he rolled over on to his stomach and pushed himself up to his hands and knees. Blood poured from his mouth and face, pooling on the sidewalk. Number 78 took the bait and punted Cor's ribs like a football. The force of the kick flipped him onto his back. He felt his ribs and sternum crack and grind against each other. Intense pain flowed from Cor's midsection. Ruptured spleen? Bruised liver maybe? Something didn't feel right to him in that area. He stared into the sky above and saw the clear blue gradually darkening with the sunset.

Brock stepped up to him, blocking his view of the sky. He grabbed him by his sweatshirt and began to pull him up again. He lifted him up a few inches but determined it wasn't worth it.

"He's like a fuckin' cripple," he said and dropped Cor back to the sidewalk.

The doors of the truck slammed shut and the engine roared. From his worm's-eye-view Cor watched the truck disappear down the street and around the corner, heading off to wherever football players go after beating up the sickly and the weak.

Cor rolled his head to the side and saw Taylor attempt to pick himself up, his breathing just beginning to return to normal.

"Next time I tell you to run, you run," Cor mumbled through the mushmouth of a broken and dislocated jaw.

Taylor made his way around the fence and rushed over to Cor's broken and bleeding body.

"Oh my God. Cor."

Taylor dug around in his backpack and pulled his cell phone out. His hands shook as he tried to command the touch screen. Cor grabbed the phone, his body flinched and tensed from the pain of his broken ribs grinding together.

"No cops," he pleaded.

"Cor, you need a doctor."

He refused to release his grip on the cell phone.

"The sun," he mumbled through his clicking jaw.

Taylor looked to the west in time to see the sun disappear below the horizon. Cor pulled the phone from Taylor's hand

and sat up. His jaw snapped back into place with a sharp, painful smack of his palm. His ribs audibly clicked, scraped and grinded as they realigned. Vision returned to his left eye. His slack cheekbone migrated under the skin back into place and the gash scabbed over.

Less than five minutes after taking the beating of a lifetime and only a few minutes after sunset Cor Griffin stood and stretched as though he had just woken from a long winter's nap.

Taylor sat motionless on the sidewalk stupefied, his mouth agape.

"You wanted proof," Cor said. He held out his hand and helped Taylor to his feet, "no cops, no doctors." He dropped Taylor's cell phone back into the backpack. The bag was loaded, seemingly, with every book that Taylor owned and a dozen or so newspapers. It must have weighed forty pounds. Cor tossed it to Taylor, nearly knocking him over.

"What was that you said about being able to kick my ass?"

21

Following the attack, Taylor walked the rest of the way to Cor's house in silence. His brilliant mind attempted and failed to make sense of what he had just witnessed. His head filled with questions he couldn't answer. At least not with an answer that was acceptable to him.

Cor left Taylor sitting at the kitchen table while he went to his room for a change of clothes. He stashed his blood soaked shirt and hoodie in a plastic bag under the bed. If Jane found them there would be too many questions. He pulled a fresh shirt and hoodie from a box marked *Cor's Clothes* and threw them on. Grabbing a box labeled *Cor's Books,* he left the bedroom.

He stopped in the hall at Jane's door and peeked in to make sure she was still sleeping. Half unpacked boxes still cluttered the floor of her room. He closed the door silently before going to the kitchen.

Taylor sat at the kitchen table, his lips moved slightly as he talked silently to himself.

"My mom is sleeping so we have to keep it down. She works the night shift." He dropped the heavy box of books on the table with a dull thud.

"Do you want a Coke or something?" Cor offered as he opened the refrigerator. Taylor didn't respond but Cor grabbed a can anyway, along with a blood bag. He snagged a couple of straws from the box on the counter.

"What the hell was that?" Taylor finally spoke his first words since Cor's recuperation after the attack.

"Those guys don't hit as hard as they think they do. They should probably lay off the roids." Cor put the soda and straw down in front of Taylor and took a seat at the table. He ripped the corner of his blood bag open, slipped the straw in and took a sip.

"No. Nope. That beating you took was the worst thing I've ever seen. And then you just get up and brush yourself off? You don't even look sick now," Taylor said and popped open the soda.

"You weren't really supposed to see that. But I did tell you that I had proof."

"Proof? Proof of what?"

"My theory."

"How is that proof of your theor— Oh. You think you're a..." Taylor's sentence trailed off and he took a long drink of his soda.

"I don't know what I am. It's not like there's a test."

"Fucking A," Taylor said. Cor was a bit surprised at the vulgarity. It was the first time he'd heard him swear. "How?" Taylor asked, returning to form.

"I don't know. I was a normal kid. I was in a car accident when I was thirteen. I lost a lot of blood. I got a transfusion. I got sick. I think the blood supply may have been tainted." Cor gave it to him straight. It was the only explanation he could think of.

"That's just not possible. Vampires don't exist. There's no scientific evidence. They're just myths. Fiction."

"All long standing myths are based on reality." Cor reached into his box of books and pulled out an old encyclopedia. The pages flipped through his fingers until he stopped on one with a post-it attached. A photo of a cave painting filled the page.

"Humans create stories based on their experiences," Cor continued, "what does every writing teacher say? *Write what you know*. This is what people have been doing since the dawn of mankind." Cor pointed out the photo.

The cave painting was a crude stick figure drawing depicting a man with large fangs biting into another man's neck. A crescent moon was drawn above the two men. Cor began pulling more books and artwork out of the box to illustrate the points he was making as he continued his speech.

"Throughout the centuries these myths continued to get resurrected. In all cultures, across every continent. They usually rose up as cautionary tales during bad times to reinforce good behavior."

"Like urban legends," Taylor interjected while flipping through some of the materials that Cor handed to him.

"Exactly. For example, the Christians distorted the myth to include crosses and holy water as a means of defense. This was to reinforce the power of the religion in the eyes of the faithful and maybe convert a few non-believers during those dark days of the middle ages. Before the ability to travel and communicate globally, these myths were all created independent of each other. Cortez arrives in South America and the natives tell him fanciful stories about blood sucking people that only come out at night and can't be killed. These stories are surprisingly similar to tales he had heard back in Europe. How would these myths have traveled there ahead of the Europeans? They didn't travel. They were created independently based on the real life experiences.

"Those were just stories. There's no scientific proof."

"Taylor, when you read something in a scientific journal, what are you reading? A story. A story about how someone believed something and then did experiments to prove it. Granted, these myths have never had the scientific process applied to them but that doesn't mean they aren't proof. Or at least theory."

"The scientific process needs consistency to prove something. It has to be the same, time after time. Test after test. These myths all have differences. There's no consistency."

"That's not really true. There is some consistency. The creatures in the myths only come out at night. They drink blood. Their bite converts other humans. There's also a general agreement about killing one too."

"A stake through the heart?"

"Kind of. That's what most people think these days but in reality the stake was only used to pin the vampire down. The killing comes through decapitation, burning or drowning. I don't think stabbing, shooting and beating will kill me but it hurts like hell. And for the record, I'm not rushing out to test what will kill me and what won't."

"So you *are* one?" Taylor asked, returning to the original topic.

"If you believe that they exist, then you would have to believe that I am one. Whatever *one* is."

"Well I don't believe it. What about going out in the sun? Aren't you supposed to burst into flames?"

"You're a scientist, you've seen evidence, yet you're still willing to dismiss it based on what happens in a movie? Bursting into flames was probably a dramatization for Hollywood. There are some depictions in historical art but those could show the burning as a means of destruction rather than the sun causing the combustion. I don't know. I'm weak in the sunlight and I don't like it. I can tell you that."

"Fine. Are you immortal? Undead? No pulse?" He asked, running through the vampire myth catalog in his head.

"Immortal? I don't know. I do age; I have grown since I was thirteen. I was declared dead and then revived after my accident, but I don't really think that counts. Pulse? I have one, it's really weak. You'd probably have trouble finding it without a heart monitor. My skin is always cold, bad circulation following the accident. I don't know. I don't have all of the answers."

"Are there more like you?"

"I've never met any that I've known of, but I have to assume there are. I'm guessing that our blood draining killer is one." Cor took the last sip of blood from the bag. Taylor noticed it for the first time.

"So, you have to drink blood? And juice boxes?"

"The juice boxes are modified. I drain the juice and refill 'em with blood."

"What's it like? Drinking blood."

"It tastes great. Think of your favorite food and multiply that by a hundred. Being around large groups of people, like at school, is tough. That's like going to a buffet when you're really hungry and not being allowed to take a bite. That's where this comes in handy." Cor patted the empty bag, "drinking the blood of my classmates would probably fall under the evil category for most people."

"And you wouldn't consider it evil? Isn't Dracula always the bad guy?"

"It's no more evil than a lion eating a person. Or a person eating a cow. For me, I need the blood of live humans. In the past, I assume, the only way to do that was to feed off of the townsfolk. What looked like murder and evil, was really just survival. Does eating a hamburger make you evil?"

"I'm a vegetarian," Taylor declared.

"Since when?"

"Since right now."

"I get it. It's freaky and scary but this is the second time today you didn't run away after I told you something insane so I gotta figure you're in one hundred percent. Or at least close to it."

"How come there isn't an epidemic of throat slashing, blood draining serial killers everywhere? Shouldn't there be some sort of evidence in every city?"

"More questions?"

"Sorry."

"These are all questions I've been asking myself for four years. The most logical answer? Self-preservation. If people knew what they were looking for, if they actually believed that I existed they would hunt me down. So I, and others like me probably, prefer to keep the myth a myth. I would bet that a lot of homeless people disappear every year. Or others do like I do." Cor got up from the table and went to the refrigerator. He opened the door to reveal dozens of blood bags hanging inside. "They raid the local blood bank. You want evidence? Every city, county and state in the U.S. has a blood supply shortage."

"Where do you get all that?" Taylor asked, his eyes wide.

"My mother is a nurse on the night shift at a hospital. She's very careful."

"She steals it? She knows about you? Is she one too?"

"She's kind of in denial. She thinks it's a dietary restriction. And no, she isn't one. As far as I know."

Taylor stood and began pacing around the room. Holding his chin in his hand, he gazed deep into the floor as though he saw through it and into the basement. Maybe he hoped something down there would help him make sense of this. Regardless of what he did or did not see on or through the floor, his mind was already made up.

"Taylor, nothing I've told you is beyond the realm of nature and known science. At this point I have to know, either you believe me and want to work toward this theory, or you don't. If you don't believe me, you can leave, and you'll never see me again."

"The throat slasher probably doesn't have access to a blood bank supply," Taylor said ignoring Cor's ultimatum.

"I think it's more than that. He could be more discrete. He does it in the open. Displays it for everyone to see. I think he knows about me. He followed me here. I think he's trying to draw me out into the open. Or maybe I'm just paranoid. Maybe it's my ego. Maybe he does it for fun. But you gotta admit, it does seem blatantly directed at me. What I do know is that the police can't stop him. I think I can."

"How?"

"If he's anything like me, we'll be evenly matched. A police officer? A dozen cops? All the bullets they have? Wouldn't stand a chance."

"Yeah, but you don't know what hurts you. Or him."

"I'll find a way. More research."

"I have an idea. Come with me to the crime lab. It's after hours. The place'll be dead. I'll run some tests." Taylor said and saw the skeptical look wash across Cor's face, "I'm a scientist. This is what I know. This is what I do. I trusted you, now you need to trust me."

22

"When CSI was number one on TV the city council thought it would be sexy to invest in a high-tech crime lab. So they took this building that was confiscated in a drug raid and bought a few pieces of equipment," Taylor explained, "When they realized they would have to raise taxes by a hundred percent to actually equip a fully functioning crime lab, they defunded it and put the money toward an underground bunker that housed an electromagnetic hydrogen bomb, called Jughead. That bomb threatens to rip apart the time-space continuum unless someone keeps entering a code and pushing a button."

Cor had no idea what Taylor was talking about but didn't interrupt for an explanation. Taylor continued, "but we still have to use the half-equipped lab and there is actually some cool high tech stuff here. Just enough so that I won't need to send any samples out for the tests that we conduct."

Taylor was right. The crime lab was dead, empty. The building had been a veterinary clinic. Originally built in the forties and maintained and operated legitimately before it became a cover for a meth lab. The clinic was a physical timeline of veterinary gear. Antiquated medical and veterinary equipment from the forties through the seventies mingled with more modern equipment from the eighties and nineties with sprinklings of meth lab supplies, current high-tech crime lab gear and computers mixed in. The tan and brown cinder block walls were evidence of the building's dual purpose as a fallout and bomb shelter during The Cold War. Most of the doors still showed the scratch mark evidence of the crime lab's previous life. It definitely lacked the shiny, neon, chrome and glass seen on TV every Wednesday night.

"Have a seat on the table," Taylor directed after flipping on the overhead fluorescent lights. The scientist, now in his element, donned a lab coat and began loading up a rolling cart with equipment and supplies.

Cor hopped up and took a seat on the stainless steel exam table. It was too small for a person to lie on comfortably, so he assumed it must be a holdover from the veterinary days. Probably for dogs, which would be more fitting if Cor were afflicted with lycanthropy.

"If anybody asks, we're just doing experiments for school," Taylor instructed as he wheeled the utensil cart over.

"Yeah. And we destroy all of the samples," Cor concurred.

"Right."

"Not a drop of blood leaves your sight," Cor emphasized the need for discretion.

"Okay, which arm?" Taylor asked.

"Does it matter?"

Cor took off his hoodie. Taylor clumsily wrapped a length of surgical tubing around Cor's right bicep. Cor tightened the tubing as Taylor fumbled around opening the alcohol wipe packaging. He wiped the crook of Cor's elbow and dropped the pad in the garbage. His hands shook as he ripped open the disposable syringe packet.

"Have you ever done this before?" Cor asked.

"Ha. Um, no. No, I have never attempted to extract blood from someone that may or may not be a vampire. Not that I know of. Um, but I can check my diary and get back to you."

"Give me that." Cor took the needle from Taylor and stuck it in his arm, jet black blood flowed into the receptacle.

"Wow. That's weird," Taylor said, stating the obvious.

"Yeah, I've never seen that."

When the first cylinder was filled Cor swapped it out and filled a second one. Once that one was full Cor pulled the needle from his arm. A bead of red blood formed at the puncture site.

"Okay." Taylor said with a hint of skepticism.

"What's next?" Cor asked. He wiped the bead of blood away from the puncture wound, which healed almost instantly.

"Um, tissue sample?" Taylor responded. He ripped the cellophane off of a Petri dish and handed a scalpel to Cor. "A finger, I guess. Just shave it thin."

Cor took the scalpel and started shaving slivers of skin from the tip of his index finger. The scalpel cut through the flesh like butter. Little disks of translucent skin flitted into the dish. Cor continued shaving through the pad of his finger until he hit bone. Taylor wobbled a little, his face went pale white and he kept his eyes averted from the procedure.

"Are you okay?" Cor asked.

"Yeah, sure. I'm just used to seeing it under a microscope. Not actually collecting the sample," Taylor said, swallowing hard.

"Right. Under a microscope. That's where you learn about life, right?" Cor teased. "Do you want a bone or marrow sample too?"

The very thought of his suggestion sent Taylor over the edge. The scientist ran from the room. Cor couldn't help himself, he snickered as the sounds of Taylor vomiting came from the hallway.

"I'll take that as a *no*," Cor called to him with a laugh.

By the time Taylor returned Cor had covered the Petri dish and bandaged his finger.

"What are you going to do about school tomorrow?" Taylor asked, "if Brock and Trey see you without bruises, they're gonna know something is up."

"Don't worry. I'll take care of Brock. What now, Dr. Frankenstein?"

"X-rays."

"Don't you need training and certification to use an x-ray machine?"

"I'm a fast learner," Taylor declared holding up a thick, yellowed book with the words VETERINARY X-RAY USERS MANUAL – 1979 written on the cover.

23

It took Taylor a couple of tries to figure out the X-ray machine but, like he said, he was a fast learner. After capturing the X-rays, Cor provided a saliva sample and left him at the lab to run the tests.

Cor's first stop was back at his house. Earlier, when he had closed his mother's bedroom door, he noticed a box labeled *Paperwork*. On top of that box was an accordion file with *Cor* written on it. He had never taken an active interest in his history or medical records but with Taylor working on things at the lab, he thought there might be documentation that could shed some light on the transfusion.

Cor set the box down on the kitchen table, unwrapped the elastic on the accordion file and began flipping through the paperwork. The file contained mostly insignificant memorabilia, report cards, academic awards, little league championship certificates and some drawings he had done in grade school. The paperwork in the file probably held some sentimental value for Jane but was virtually worthless to Cor. Until he came across his birth certificate.

He had never seen his birth certificate before, had never cared to. As he pulled the official document from the file, he immediately noticed something was very, very wrong. The birth certificate was a registered legal document from the State of Washington. Cor's place of birth was listed as:

MEMORIAL HOSPITAL, SEATTLE, WA

His name was listed correctly:

CORDELL BLAKELY GRIFFIN

For *Mother's Name*, typed and signed on the line was:

JANE CORDELL

That doesn't make sense. Cor's mother had always claimed that her name was Griffin.

Next to her name, the spot for *Father's Name* should have been a blank line. Jane had always maintained that Cor's father took off as soon as she told him she was pregnant. That field should have nothing. Maybe a row of X's typed through it. Or *UNKNOWN*. Instead, the information listed there put an end to the biggest lie of Cordell Griffin's life:

FATHER'S NAME: BLAKELY GRIFFIN

And it was signed.

24

For the better part of an hour Cor's reflection stared blankly back at him from the surface of the dark, cool cup of coffee. Gazing into the cup of coffee answered as many of his questions as staring into the dark night sky the hour before. Cor had fled his house before succumbing to the urge to tear through every last box in an attempt to uncover more of Jane's lies. He hoped to find The Creeper at the diner. That wish evaporated when he arrived, the diner was deserted.

That's what happens when word gets out that a serial killer is in the neighborhood. Everyone locks their doors, closes their shutters and stays inside after dark. Nine months later the local maternity ward will likely be busy.

With The Creeper's absence Cor forced himself to believe that the pattern had been broken. That maybe The Creeper had moved on, or retired, or died. Maybe there was no connection between him and the killings. Maybe he wanted to be part of something bigger. Maybe he actually wanted to be part of the world he was disconnected from. The world that he preferred to remain invisible to. Maybe The Creeper wasn't even the killer. Maybe in tomorrow's newspaper he wouldn't find out that he was wrong.

Too many maybes.

The bell above the door chimed as a pair of foot patrol police officers came in from the dark. The local PD had increased patrols in an attempt to get a handle on the situation and reassure people that the streets were safe.

The two cops bellied up to the counter. The sole waitress on duty reflexively set out two mugs and started pouring coffee. Small talk ensued, mostly revolving around the words murder, serial and killer.

Cor took this as his cue to leave. The cops might not appreciate a high school kid out at two AM on a school night. They might have questions for him. He dropped five bucks on the table, grabbed his backpack and slid out of the booth. The cops were busy fixing up their coffees and didn't notice as he slinked by.

Cor wrapped his hand around the bell above the door and pulled it to the side to keep it from ringing as he opened the door. He slipped silently out without catching their eye or raising suspicions. The waitress might be able to give a description of him, but it would be fuzzy. Cor had seen her shooting nips in the kitchen.

He trotted down the few steps from the diner and crossed the sidewalk to the curb. He looked both ways before crossing the street. That was when he saw him.

He stood under a streetlight, two blocks up in the direction of Odel Park, staring back at Cor. Cor considered ignoring him. He considered not playing this game.

What if I walked away, went home and got in bed? Who would The Creeper play with then?

But he only entertained that idea for a split second before turning up the street toward him. The Creeper immediately disappeared behind the corner of a house down a cross street when Cor made his move toward him.

Cor broke into a full sprint. During the daylight hours Cor could barely walk, his body constantly revolting against him. After sundown, he was twice as fast as any gold medal sprinter.

He got to the corner and rounded it, ducking into a shadow. He had to be extra careful with the increase in police patrols. Up the road The Creeper maintained the two-block distance between the two of them. Cor was convinced now, The Creeper could definitely move at the same speed.

He's got what I've got.

Cor gave chase again, sprinting the two blocks only to have The Creeper disappear around another corner. He caught a final glimpse as The Creeper faded into the depths of Odel Park.

Cor dashed across the street, past the wrought iron gate and into the darkness. The Creeper was nowhere to be seen. Vanished again.

Cor stepped off the pathway into the much darker, shaded woods. Cor was determined. He wouldn't leave the park tonight until he found him.

25

Cor searched the acres of trails, a playground with swing sets, and the stretches of woods in between and turned up empty. He emerged from a thin path at the far end of the wooded park. The path opened up to a mid sized parks and rec athletic field. A soccer goal stood alone at the far end of the field to the right. A couple of picnic tables were haphazardly placed along the edge, near the gravel parking lot across the field from him.

He lurked in the darkness of the tree line for a few minutes observing the stillness of the empty field. He looked for movement or anything out of the ordinary. Other than the bright blue, jacked up 4x4 pickup truck in the gravel parking lot, nothing seemed out of place.

He took his time circling the perimeter of the field. It was safer than exposing himself by walking across the field in the bright moonlight. He kept his eyes on the truck while cautiously and silently making his way around to the edge of the parking lot. He was certain that The Creeper had led him to it.

The engine wasn't running. A fine layer of dew had settled over the windows and the body of the truck. Cor eased up along the passenger side. He swiped his hand across the glass clearing the dew from the window and saw her.

Caitlyn was in the passenger seat. Her body was slumped against the door. Her light hair lay limply across the pale skin of her face.

Anger welled up in Cor's throat. The Creeper had struck again! This time though, it wasn't some random person that had fatally bumped into the wrong guy. This time he had struck closer than ever before. This time he had gotten to someone that Cor cared about. His fists clenched tightly and tears welled up in his eyes. Tonight would be the night, no more tests, no more research. Now was the time to kill The Creeper.

Cor drove his fist into the door of the truck, making a dent the size of a grapefruit. The loud clang and quaking of the truck jolted Caitlyn. She sprang awake and screamed.

"Oh my God!" She slapped the door locks down and leapt to the driver's side to get away from whoever was outside. She ripped open her backpack and fumbled for her cell phone in the relative darkness.

Cor wiped his hand against the glass to clear away more of the dew. He brought his face close to the window so she could see him. She glanced up right before pressing the send button and recognized Cor.

"Caitlyn, are you okay?" Cor shouted through the glass.

"Cor?"

"Yeah. Are you okay?"

She scooted back across the seat and opened the door.

"Oh my God, you scared me to death," Caitlyn let out a heavy breath of relief. Cor could see her pulse pounding in her throat. He could have stared at the rhythmic beat for an eternity.

"What are you doing in Brock's truck?" He asked her.

"This is Trace's truck. We were supposed to study but he came here to get drunk with his friends instead."

"Here?"

"Yeah, they were playing football or something. They're probably passed out somewhere. What time is it?"

Cor scanned the field. He didn't see anybody out there. "About 2:30 in the morning."

"My father is going to freakin' kill me! Where the heck is Trace?"

"I don't know. I haven't seen him around, but it's not safe for you here. I can walk you home."

"I live way on the other side of town."

"That's okay, it can't be more than five or six miles. It's a nice night for a walk. Besides, it'll give you an extra hour or so before your father kills you."

26

At three AM Cor and Caitlyn had the streets to themselves. For most of the walk they strolled along slowly. Cor hoped she was keeping the leisurely pace to extend the time they spent together. The night sky was clear and the stars shone above. The moon hung low in the early morning hours.

Under different circumstances it might have been a romantic night to remember. The kind of thing that only happens in movies. Like strolling through the streets of Prague getting to know someone he just met on a train. Unfortunately, Cor didn't have the luxury of turning this walk into a relationship. His top priority was to get Caitlyn home safe. In the back of his mind he had a strong feeling that he would find Trace on the front page of the morning newspapers. But for tonight, his focus was to get Caitlyn home safely, not take her on a romantic moonlit stroll.

As they passed through the night, traveling further from Cor's neighborhood, the houses got bigger, the grass grew greener and every step brought them closer to their goodbye. Cor cherished the limited amount of time he had in her presence, walking side by side, often in silence. Occasionally their hands would brush. He was sure it happened by accident but hoped, that Caitlyn had intentionally swung her hand slightly toward his.

He felt great. Normal. Not sick. Not hindered with illness or wracked with weakness. He was able to stand straight and walk tall without wheezing. A sinking feeling pervaded the back of his mind. A feeling that this may be the only time Caitlyn would see him this way. When the sun rose, and for the rest of the days that he would know her, she would only see a pale, feeble, sick kid.

He stole a glance at her from the corner of his eye. She walked at ease alongside him, comfortable to be walking with him in silence. There was no need to cloud the air with senseless babble or unnecessary filler. No need to be constantly doing something. No cell phones, no texting. Just walking beside each other, sharing their time together, was enough.

Cor noticed that her pace slowed. They must have been getting close to her house. He could feel the change in her demeanor. Fear and anticipation were creeping in. Since beginning the walk something seemed to be on the tip of her tongue. She seemed to have something to tell him, but she held back. Her nervousness increased and her breaths shortened. If she had something to say, she would have to say it soon.

They turned onto Ocean Avenue and Caitlyn finally spoke, "I can't get that song out of my head, you know," she said softly, not wanting to shatter the calm of the quiet night.

"What?" Cor's voice cracked.

"The song you played. The other day."

"It's not really done yet. I actually wrote another verse after playing it for you." He didn't mean to admit that he had, in fact, played it specifically for her that day. They walked a few feet in silence between their statements, nervous about the impact of each word. Of each confession.

"I tried to learn it," She said and blushed, "I know. I'm a dork."

Her revelation took Cor by surprise. Of everything that he had learned tonight, this was the most stunning. He froze, stopped walking, partly to make sure that he understood her. Partly to extend his time with her in this night on Earth.

"I don't know what to say."

"What?" She stopped and turned to face him, "I'm sorry," and she turned away again, "I can't get it anyway."

Cor jogged a couple of steps to catch up.

"No, don't apologize. That's the biggest compliment you could give me. I'm truly appreciative of that."

The two of them stood less than a foot apart. The white mist from her exhalation, visible in the cool early morning air, swirled and blended with his dark, invisible breath into a churning cloud between them. He looked down into her face, her perfect, smooth, innocent pale skin. He filled with wonder at the thought of this girl. She epitomized everything good, she had everything she wanted or needed; yet she was touched by the words that he had written. He could never hope for a greater success.

As the wonder filled his face he could see the embarrassment of her confession fade, replaced with expectation for what may come in this moment between them.

Their eyes met for the first time. Their bodies remained unmoving; the swirling cloud between them disappeared as her breath paused in anticipation. Cor could feel her pure white soul drawn to the vacuum between them by the gravity of his dark matter heart.

It was only then that he realized the magnitude of the danger he had placed her in. His very existence had endangered the most pure and beautiful essence he'd ever experienced. Earlier tonight he thought that Caitlyn had been killed because of his relationship with her. As long as that danger still existed he refused to risk her safety. Cor turned away and took the first heavy steps toward the last leg of their journey. It took Caitlyn a few seconds, but she followed behind him and caught up.

"My father must have thought I was crazy. I haven't touched the piano since I was seven," She said after walking a few minutes in silence. It was chatter, just something that filled the uncomfortable void.

They continued on in silence past a dozen or more big houses with big lawns.

"This is me," she said, stopping to let Cor know he had fulfilled his duty to bring her home safely.

"Okay," was all Cor could muster.

They both knew what was meant to be and what never will. Things had changed forever, irrevocably and dangerously.

"Thank you for walking me home," she whispered politely, "I wouldn't mind doing it again sometime. If I'm not grounded forever."

Cor remained silent, unsure of how to respond to the melancholy in her voice. On the surface, her sadness may have been a reflection of the fate she feared awaited behind the front door of her house. Deeper down, the sorrow in her brilliant soul was the same ache that penetrated Cor's dark, once still heart. The ache warned them both that they might never realize the potential they felt on this cool November night. Cor's pain manifested a little deeper, fueled by the belief that he had doomed her.

He focused on a blade of grass at her feet, fearful that eye contact might create something too powerful to resist.

"Good night Cor," she said softly and turned toward the house.

He grabbed her arm and turned her back toward him. He leaned in close to her neck, right below her right ear. Her pulse throbbed under the thin, smooth skin of her neck.

"There is a danger out there. Promise me that you will not spend a minute alone," he whispered into her ear.

She drew in a quivering breath.

"Promise me."

She understood and nodded. Cor released his grip on her arm. His mouth hovered, millimeters from her neck. She hesitated. He inhaled deeply, pulling her succulent scent into his nose and then he turned his lips away. She exhaled and started the walk across the wet, perfectly trimmed grass. When she got to the door, she turned, to see him one last time but he was already gone.

He crouched in the shadows three houses down and watched the door close after Caitlyn disappeared into her house.

Cor stayed there until dawn.

27

The overcast sky and light mist in the air did little to ease Cor's sickening weakness. He trudged through the school parking lot with his hood up, head down and fists jammed in his pockets. He hoped, in the light of day, that classes with Caitlyn wouldn't be too awkward. After leaving her house this morning he barely had enough time to get home, pack a few modified drink boxes and grab his books.

Taylor intercepted him about halfway across the parking lot. He was more excited than normal.

"Cor! Cor!" He called his name out breathlessly in a loud, hoarse whisper. "You can't go in there." He grabbed Cor by the arm and dragged him between a pair of vans. "Did you see this? Did you SEE this?" Taylor could barely contain himself as he shoved a newspaper in Cor's face. "You didn't really mean you were going to *take care* of Brock, did you?"

"What are you talking about?" Cor took the paper from Taylor.

"The latest victim," Taylor started but didn't need to finish. The front page of the newspaper had a quarter-page photo of Brock holding a football and a headline that read:

LOCAL HIGH SCHOOL FOOTBALL STAR FOUND DEAD IN ODEL PARK

"This is bad."

"No kidding, Cor. The police are here interviewing everybody that might know something. Friends. Enemies. The whole school knows he choked you out the other day. That's motive right there. Kids have been speculating about you all morning. Everybody thinks you did it."

"I was in the park last night."

"What?"

"I followed The Creeper. He led me to the park and I lost him."

"Did anyone see you?"

"Yeah. It makes sense now. He led me into the park to find Brock. To place me at his murder. Maybe even while he did it. I didn't find Brock." Cor hesitated to tell him the next part. "I found Caitlyn. Asleep in Trace's truck. I made sure she got home safely."

"This is bad."

"Yeah. Shit! I thought The Creeper was leading me to her. As a threat. He might not have even known she was there."

"This is bad," Taylor repeated, "the police are going to talk to her. And they're going to talk to you. You shouldn't be here today."

"They'll think I'm guilty. I'd rather voluntarily talk to them here and buy some time, rather than have them take me down to the station. I don't have anything to hide."

"Yeah, you do." Taylor pulled a folder out of his backpack and handed it to Cor. "Your test results."

Cor took the folder. "I meant about the murder. Is there anything in here that will help us?"

"I think so."

"Let's get inside and talk, I don't like hanging around out here."

28

Every student they passed stole a glance in Cor's direction. Despite their attempts at discretion, Cor could see the finger pointing and hear the whispering. The crowds parted and kids moved aside, turning and looking over their shoulders as the two of them walked through the halls. Mr. Gifford's classroom was empty so Cor and Taylor ducked in and closed the door behind them.

Cor opened the folder and laid it out on a table. The documents inside were filled with technical terms and scientific gibberish.

"What am I looking at?" Cor asked.

"That's what I said when I first looked through the microscope. These are the test results from a previously, completely unrecorded biology. Oh, and before we get into all of this, let me just tell you now, I am all in. Whatever art or story or myth you tell me, I'm behind it and you one hundred percent. To put it bluntly, this is the coolest thing I've ever seen and some seriously freaky shit. No offense."

"None taken."

"I don't have the capabilities at the crime lab to map the DNA and really get into the chemical and biological compounds so I decided to do some basic tests and also test the major vampire myths against it. First thing. Your blood is black, until it hits air, then it turns red. I have no idea why. That'll take some more testing. Just don't let anyone draw blood from you in the meantime." He flipped the page. "Garlic. Your sample had a very negative reaction."

"Okay."

"Silver. More commonly used in myth to kill werewolves, which, by the way, if you come across some artwork that convinces you werewolves exist, you have to tell me immediately. Those things scare the heck out of me."

"Duly noted."

"Okay, back to silver. Used to kill werewolves, but vampires are commonly believed to not have reflections. That would mean that they weren't visible in mirrors, which were traditionally made of polished silver. Also, vampires can't be photographed on film, which is silver based. And you mentioned that silver as a weapon has come around recently. Possibly because in the distant past it wasn't cost effective to make a silver sword which would be useless in a regular battle.

"Okay, I get it. How did my sample do against silver?"

"Bad. Stay away from silver knives and bullets."

"Will do."

"Moving on. Sunlight. The visible spectrum caused no ill effects. UV on the other hand destroyed the small sample. How do you feel today?"

"Shitty."

Exactly. UV radiation penetrates clouds and mist to a lesser degree, but it still gets through. It isn't sunlight that hurts you, it's the UV.

"Great."

"Yeah, so much for two hundred and forty overcast days. Your best bet is to stock up on sunblock or live in a rainforest with a thick canopy. Or not to leave the house during the day."

"Maybe I should get a coffin to sleep in. I tried sunblock in L.A. Didn't work."

"Okay, Might be more than just UV. We'll need more tests. Moving on. What do all of these have in common?" Taylor asked.

"I don't know."

"They're all biological cleansers. Garlic is well known to have very good blood cleansing capabilities. There's an alternative treatment called colloidal silver, where microscopic silver particles are suspended in water and used as medicine. The silver is pure. It cleans pathogens and toxins from your system. Well not *your* system but, um, normal people's systems." Taylor stumbled a little referring to normal people. "That didn't offend you, did it?"

"No, not at all."

"Okay, anyway, this might explain the holy water thing. If holy water was stored in silver flasks or containers the silver might have leached or flecked into the water and, voila, colloidal silver. UV rays are also a purifier. We use them in the lab to sterilize equipment. You'll also find that doctors and dentists do the same. Basically you're like a virus."

"Now that, I find offensive." Cor joked.

"Oh, I'm sorry, I didn't mean to..." Taylor stuttered, missing the joke.

"I'm kidding. So this is how we kill The Creeper?"

"It doesn't seem that any of these alone is enough to outright kill you. They definitely slow or stop some of the other unique properties of your cells. In large enough quantities, maybe dipped in a vat of garlic or molten silver or standing under the hole in the Ozone you would perish. Which makes me wonder what Australian vampires are doing since the Ozone depletion there is higher than elsewhere. Do they just migrate around hoping to avoid the movement of the hole? I mean their habitat is shrinking. It's like the pandas in China..."

"Taylor," Cor cut him off, "can we worry about Australia and the pandas later?"

"Sorry. Basically, you're a different, previously undiscovered animal. With more time, more equipment and more tests - stem cells and DNA would be at the top of my list - we could learn so much more."

"Short of dissecting me though, we have to rely on historical evidence for killing someone else like me. Is that what you're saying?"

"Yes, if The Creeper is actually the same thing as you."

"I chased him last night. He's faster than I am. I'm sure he's the same. Back to killing him. Decapitation, burning and drowning should work according to historical evidence. Any verification of the wooden stake?"

"Wood by itself has no effect. I tested a few different kinds and nothing registered. I think you were right about the stake being used to pin the vampire down. Let me see your finger." Cor showed Taylor the finger he skinned the tissue sample from. It was completely healed.

"Your cells regenerate thousands of times faster than normal human cells. Burning will kill you if you burn faster than your cells heal, and your cells still require oxygen so drowning will kill you too, but it'll take awhile. Throw in garlic, silver and UV and it messes up your regeneration and replication cell properties. For example, if you were to take a massive beating while your body is fighting off UV rays you're going to take a lot of damage, and probably won't heal from it until you get out of the UV, but it's unlikely you'll die from that."

"Just for example, right?"

Taylor smirked.

"Did the X-rays show anything?"

"Despite the poor quality, which I blame on operator malfunction, I was able to make some neat discoveries," he said, a bit too giddy. "Your bone structure is fairly normal. With a few notable exceptions."

"Such as?"

"You have fangs," Taylor said.

"Bullshit."

"Seriously, look."

"I've never had fangs."

"Actually, it's just your canine teeth, but look."

Cor held the X-ray up to the fluorescent light. He saw what Taylor called fangs. His canine teeth extended into his gumline much further than the rest of his teeth.

"They appear to be recessed," Taylor continued, "like a cat's claw. Like they can pop out."

"How? They've never popped out."

"Maybe you haven't needed them? I could never wiggle my ear until I needed to."

"Really Taylor?"

"Never mind. The point is, now that you know they are there, maybe you can focus on them and make them work. But I have to warn you, be very, very careful who you bite. Look here." Taylor pointed to a pair of large dark areas just above the canine teeth in the X-ray.

"What are those?" Cor asked.

"They're kind of like really big sinus cavities. The same type of cavity can be found in a lot of snakes. Venomous snakes to be exact."

"Venomous?"

"Yes. My theory is that vampirism is spread through a poisonous bite. Not through saliva and not through blood. I mixed your blood sample with a normal blood sample. Your blood did not infect or assimilate the normal blood at all. In fact, they separated like oil and water. Vampirism doesn't spread like a virus.

"What about the blood transfusion?"

"That's the thing. There's no way that your blood could pass even the simplest, archaic blood screening system. It would never be considered human blood and would never make it into the blood supply. It would be like trying to donate cherry Kool-aid at the blood drive. And furthermore, if you were human and were given vampire blood in a transfusion, your body would reject it outright. I am one hundred percent positive that you did not become a vampire from a blood transfusion."

"But I was never sick before the accident."

"I'm questioning whether or not you even had a transfusion."

"It wouldn't be the biggest lie my mother ever told me."

"Hear me out," Taylor said, "based on the tests that I did we can rule out transfusion as a means of becoming a vampire. That only leaves bite, which I can't really be sure of because I didn't test the venom in those sinus cavities so I don't know what it does. It is possible that a venomous bite could alter your biological or chemical makeup but I can't imagine a poison altering your bone structure or making you grow fangs, which makes a bite even more questionable."

"How then?"

"You were born with it."

"No way. I was normal before the accident." Cor protested.

"Which happened right as you were reaching puberty. Based on the tests, I have a theory that vampirism affects you as you mature. The same way a normal human's body changes. The cells didn't grow, age or reproduce at the same rate under the microscope. They grew at an inverse exponential rate. Continually slower growth, atrophy and decay. Unlike human cells, which steadily grow old and die, your cells grow slow. You don't age the same as a human. Currently you're keeping pace with me, but when you reach full adulthood, between 24 and 30, you will stop. Or at least slow down to an imperceptible rate. I don't know if you're immortal, but a natural death won't come to you for a couple hundred years. Maybe more."

"I inherited this?"

"What do you know about your father?"

"Before ten hours ago? Nothing. My mother always said that he took off when she first told him she was pregnant. Last night, I found this." Cor pulled the birth certificate out of his backpack and handed it to Taylor.

"I thought you were from California?" Taylor questioned immediately.

"So did I. And look," Cor pointed to the Blakely Griffin name and signature. "My father didn't desert us. He was there when I was born. We left him." Cor didn't bother to mention the discrepancy with his mother's name.

"Do you know what this means?"

"My father is a vampire, and our number one suspect."

"And you thought you were just a normal kid."

"Yeah."

"Another theory that I have is that there's a vast vampire underground or secret society. When you were brought into the hospital after your accident your tests would have definitely raised an eyebrow. The doctors that worked on you would have had to cover it up. I bet even your birth was covered up by the vampires. This attending physician, Dr. Sullivan," He reads from the birth certificate, "was probably in on it too. Do you remember anything from the accident?"

"Not really. A few bits and pieces. Supposedly I died and was revived."

"I have one last theory to float past you."

"Okay."

"The two most influential rock musicians of the past 60 years are alive. And are vampires."

"What?" Cor asked, questioning Taylor's sanity.

"Elvis Presley and Kurt Cobain. Tupac might be one too but I didn't have time to fully look into the mystery surrounding his supposed death. Look."

Taylor pulled two massive files from his backpack. One was labeled:

KURT

The other was:

ELVIS

"You did all this last night?" Cor asked, dumbfounded.

"Yes," he replied as if that was a strange question.

"Have you slept? How much coffee did you drink?"

"No, to the first. 1.34 gallons to the second. I'm due for a venti right about now."

"You're not a normal kid either, you know."

Taylor smirked at the compliment as the two of them headed out into the hall. Neither of them saw Mr. Gifford emerge from a storage closet in the classroom.

29

All first period classes were canceled. The entire student body was assembled in the gymnasium where an official announcement about Brock's death was made. The rest of the hour was made available for students to console each other. Teachers and counselors were on hand to offer support and comfort.

During the announcement Principal Dupris instructed the students that classes would resume as scheduled. Due to the circumstances surrounding Brock's death the police were interested in speaking with some students. They would need all of the students to follow their regular schedule so that they could be found when needed.

Cor's nerves were on edge. Caitlyn and Trace weren't at the assembly and Taylor was a twitchy mess of paranoia, compounded by a lack of sleep and an overdose of caffeine.

After the assembly Cor told him to go to the library, hide in a corner and take a nap. He assured Taylor that he would find him if anything happened.

30

Caitlyn was already sitting at the table in Mr. Gifford's classroom when Cor arrived. He took his seat next to her, which was a mixed blessing. With no barrier between them he still felt a residual gravitational pull from last night. But he wouldn't have to make eye contact.

"Are you okay?" He asked quietly, "I didn't see you at the assembly." Cor was sincere but afraid his words sounded forced.

"Yeah. I overslept."

The air between them was heavy and uncomfortable. Cor pulled his art history book from his backpack, put it on the table and opened it. He knew they wouldn't be having a regular class, but it gave him something to focus on.

"He's the first person I've known that died," Caitlyn said softly.

Actually he's not, Cor thought but responded "It's a waste of potential when someone young dies," instead.

"That's nice of you to say Cor. Especially after the way he treated you."

"I have to hope that if he had been given the chance, he would have made things right," Cor said it but wasn't sure if he believed it. "How's Trace?"

"Not good. He called to tell me this morning. Said he woke up in the park and Brock was gone. It could have been me, Cor. I was in the park too."

So was I, Cor thought, wondering if Caitlyn might jump to the conclusion that he could be a suspect.

"Have you talked to the police?"

"Not yet."

Mr. Gifford entered the classroom and moved to the head of the class to make an announcement.

"You all know by now what happened to Brock Reynolds." He started walking from desk to desk as he spoke. "To some of you he was a friend. To others he was just a classmate or one of your school's football players. I think that we can all agree that regardless of what you thought of him, his life was cut short. The death of another human being is never something to take lightly. We only get one chance on this planet and if we live to be a hundred years old, it still might not be long enough to do everything that must be done. Some of you may be called to talk to the police today. I want you to know that if any of you..." Mr. Gifford stopped at Cor's table, "...any of you need anything at all while being interviewed, stop the interview and have them call me immediately." He placed a Principal's Office Call Slip on the table in front of Cor.

"They would like to see you in the office."

He expected this would be coming sooner rather than later.

"See you later?" Cor asked Caitlyn.

"Definitely."

31

Principal Dupris' office hadn't changed since Cor first sat there with his mother two days ago. He sat in the same chair, alone in the office waiting for his interview to begin. The door opened and Dupris entered followed by two other men. All three could have been detectives. They wore similar dark, plain grey suits, cheap ties and carried themselves with an air of entitlement. The only difference was that Dupris didn't have a badge or holster prominently displayed on his belt. He Dupris took his jacket off and draped it over the back of his leather throne before sitting.

"Cor, this is Detective Orlovsky," Principal Dupris indicated the bigger of the two detectives. Orlovsky had a dark crew cut and thick mustache. He half took a seat on the front left corner of Dupris' desk, settling the left half of his sizeable ass on the glossy mahogany wood and draping his leg, bent at the knee, over the front of the desk. His raised shin nearly touched Cor's knee. Orlovsky held a Styrofoam fast-food coffee cup in his hand like it was a beer bottle. His stomach bulged prominently over his belt, partially obscuring his badge.

"And this is Detective Tolliver," Dupris indicated to the other man. Tolliver was probably fifteen years younger than

Orlovsky and more fit. The years of donut fueled stakeouts hadn't yet taken their toll on his physique. He had wispy blonde hair, parted on the side and already a bit grey around the ears. He circled around behind Cor and remained standing in the corner to the right of Dupris' desk. He had a small notepad and a pen at the ready.

"Do you know why you're here?" Orlovsky started the questioning.

"Principal Dupris said the police would be asking us about Brock. So I assume that's what it's for."

"That's correct. Do you want your mother present? If not, Principal Dupris can observe in her place," Detective Tolliver said.

"That's fine. She works nights. I'm sure she's sleeping now." Cor knew that Dupris wasn't going to protect his best interests but Jane would have made a scene. Cor grew increasingly uncomfortable in the situation. It was impossible for him to be invisible with three pairs of eyes on him. He slumped in the chair.

"Are you nervous. Cor?" Dupris asked. Cor thought he heard a touch of hope in Dupris voice. He figured the principal was wishing that he was scared shitless without a father figure to guide him.

"No. Should I be?" Cor responded, the defiance clear in his voice.

"Absolutely not. We just have a few questions," Tolliver chimed in. From where Cor was sitting it looked like they were going to play 'Good Cop, Good Cop,' but he couldn't figure out where 'Bad Principal' fit into the game.

"We've been hearing from other students that you had an altercation with Brock Reynolds in the hallway, the day before yesterday. Can you tell me about that?" Orlovsky asked, getting straight to the point.

"Not much to tell. I'm the new kid. Maybe he had a point to make. Very forcefully. Nothing major really. He was probably just playing around."

"Some of the witnesses said that you..." Tolliver flipped a page in his notepad and read from it, "...collapsed to the floor after Brock released a choke hold. Choking someone out doesn't seem like playing around, to me. And this was your first day?"

"Any problems at your previous school?" Orlovsky asked, without allowing Cor a chance to answer Tolliver's question.

"Where were you at approximately 2:30 this morning?" Tolliver fired the next question off. Cor quickly determined that the interview had descended into a 'Bad Cop, Bad Cop' interrogation. They were trying to throw him off. Scare him. Confuse him. Make him answer without thinking. Cor had been through enough of these interviews in Los Angeles to know the drill.

"Answer the questions, Cor," Dupris jumped in on the power trip, just as Cor thought he would.

"Are you okay?" Tolliver asked, noticing Cor slumping further into the chair.

"No, not really. I'm sick. I'm always sick." Cor embellished it a little to play up his feebleness. It didn't take much to look like he was dying.

"That's on record. No sports," Dupris informed his new buddies.

"What prompted the altercation?" Orlovsky asked, getting back to the original line of questioning, and with a softer tone of voice.

Cor knew that the response Orlovsky was looking for would be *which altercation the one where he choked me or the one where I killed him?* Instead Cor responded calmly.

"Brock told me to stay away from a certain girl."

"Which girl?" Dupris butted in, a little too interested in the details.

"Principal Dupris, we'll ask the questions." Detective Tolliver put him in his place. "Any trouble at your previous school?"

"No more than any other kid. You can check my transcripts."

"We did," Orlovsky said, but Cor already knew that. "Academically, very impressive. Behaviorally you had some problems." This was nothing new.

"You should probably tell us now if your name is going to come up connected to similar murders involving classmates in Los Angeles." Tolliver's request hit Cor like a sucker punch from left field. His knuckles went white as his grip tightened around the wooden arm rests of the chair.

"Similar to what?" He asked through a clenched jaw.

"Why didn't you report the altercation?" Orlovsky asked.

"Which altercation?" Cor asked back without thinking. He immediately regretted it and Tolliver pounced on the opening.

"There was more than one?" He asked and shot a look at Orlovsky.

Cor tried to clear his head. His mind was focused on the Los Angeles case files with his name all over them.

"Yeah, we uh," he stuttered back, "we, uh, talked in the cafeteria earlier in the day. None of your witnesses mentioned that? Everybody was there." Cor hoped that would cover his bases for the time being and keep the detectives from jumping to conclusions.

"You didn't report either incident?" Orlovsky asked.

"It was my first day here. He was laying down the law. Nothing out of the ordinary. I'm sure I'm not the only one he did it to." Cor's breathing became labored. He was having trouble focusing. One thought filled his mind

I have to get out of here before those files arrive.

"Where were you at 2:30 this morning?" Tolliver asked.

"I was home in bed," Cor replied coolly.

"That's a lie!" Dupris burst out. "He brought my daughter home at four AM." The Principal leaned back in his big leather chair and put his hands behind his head, very satisfied with himself. Armpit stains flanked each side of his smug face.

"Your daughter?" Cor blurted out, sucker punched again.

"Yes, Cor. Caitlyn Dupris is my daughter," he said with a chuckle.

"That's enough Dr. Dupris," Orlovsky reprimanded him. "Cor, we're done for now but we're going to need to talk to you again later. Make sure you don't leave school grounds. And you might want to call your mother."

32

Cor left Dupris' office and went straight to his locker, to ditch his books. Taylor was right, he shouldn't have come to school today. The police were too close. He needed to get out of there. He needed to run. He needed to hide. And he needed to stop The Creeper tonight.

He had enough trouble walking normally with a backpack full of books. With only the cooler and drink boxes the backpack would be much lighter and wouldn't slow him down as much. As he dumped his books in the locker a uniformed policeman passed him in the hall. The officer carried a cardboard file box with the L.A.P.D. crest stamped on the side. He was heading toward Principal Dupris' office.

After the officer passed him, Cor took off toward the exit in the opposite direction. At the door he took a quick glance back down the hall to make sure it was clear. His hands pressed on the panic bar and the door swung open. He froze. An unmarked police cruiser was parked right outside. He hadn't seen the car through the door's thin vertical window but now stood in full view of it and the undercover officer inside. He grabbed at the bar and quickly pulled the door closed.

"Damn." Cor had to rethink his escape plan. He had to get Taylor.

Cor would have to pass the Principal's Office in order to get to the library. He shuffled down the hall as fast as possible, sucking breath in and wheezing back out. As he approached the door he slowed to a normal walk but kept his face turned away from the door as he passed. Walking blindly forward he collided with someone exiting the office. Cor stumbled and staggered from the impact but didn't turn toward the office or whoever he hit. He mumbled an apology without looking and attempted to continue on to the library.

"Cor?" Caitlyn asked. He had run into the principal's daughter.

"Caitlyn?" He responded in surprise. Glancing over his shoulder at her he picked up the pace and shuffle-limped as fast as he could. "I have to go," he wheezed.

She jogged to catch up to him, "Cor, I just heard the police talking. They have some files from L.A. They think you killed Brock."

"I know. I didn't do it," Cor said, gasping between each word, "you have to believe me."

"I do. They're going to arrest you."

"Caitlyn, I can't let that happen. They won't understand. If I go to jail, I'll die. I have to get out of here."

"Where are you going?"

"I have to get Taylor, he's in the library."

Caitlyn grabbed his hand and started pulling him down the hall.

"Come on, we don't have much time."

33

Cor fell into the table, startling Taylor. The genius had been sleeping, face down in a biography of Tupac Shakur. Taylor bolted upright, shocked out of his dream world. His glasses crooked on his face and a smear of drool running across his cheek. Cor was completely winded and couldn't speak. He dropped into a seat at the table.

"Taylor, we need to get Cor out of here." Caitlyn said.

"Huh? What?" Taylor couldn't figure out what planet he was on, never mind why Caitlyn Dupris was talking to him. He wiped his cheek off with his sleeve. "Great."

"Right now! Cor is in trouble, Taylor."

"The police?" Taylor asked coming to his senses.

"You know?"

"File from L.A," Cor wheezed, hoping Taylor would understand the gravity of the situation.

"Damn," Taylor swore under his breath, "it got here quicker than I thought. I found out that one of the uniformed cops just transferred from the L.A.P.D. He noticed some off-the-record similarities and mentioned it. I didn't think it would get here til tomorrow."

"My name is all over those reports, Taylor. I was a person of interest in L.A." Cor confessed breathlessly.

"What?"

"I know. I should have told you. I have to get out of here."

"I'm coming with you," Caitlyn informed the two boys.

"No, I don't want you involved. I don't want you getting hurt." Cor stood to leave. Taylor grabbed his sleeve and easily pulled him back down to the chair.

"I'm already involved," Taylor and Caitlyn said in unison.

"We're running out of time," Caitlyn informed them, "if we get to the loading dock of the cafeteria my car is parked out back."

"No. It's too dangerous," Cor protested.

"You can't do this alone," Taylor declared, slinging his backpack over his shoulders.

"We have to go now. They're going to be looking for you. You're not leaving here without us Cor. We won't let them take you."

"Caitlyn, how do you know I'm innocent?"

"You know how I know. I felt it last night. You have a good heart, Cor."

"We have to go!" Taylor grabbed Cor's arm and lifted him out of the chair. He wrapped Cor's arm around the back of his neck and supported his weight the best he could.

"Take him to the back door in the cafeteria. Meet me at my car. It's a powder blue VW Bug near the loading dock at the kitchen. I'll try to distract the detectives and meet you there," Caitlyn said.

The three of them made their way out of the library and into the empty hallway where they split up, Taylor and Cor headed for the cafeteria, Caitlyn dashed off toward the Principal's Office.

34

Cor could barely move. His energy had almost fully deserted him as Taylor dragged him down the hall. Without Taylor's help he would have been crawling along the floor.

The two boys entered the empty cafeteria. The bell was only a few minutes away. Once it rang, every kid in the school would fill the lunchroom.

Cor glanced down the hallway behind them. Caitlyn intercepted her father's secretary and Detective Tolliver. Time was running out.

Taylor dragged his friend to the back door. Cor's feet barely caught under him to help lighten the load. Taylor was slowing down. His breathing and heartbeat were increasing. He didn't have much left in the tank. He was about to push open the back door when Cor grabbed his hand.

"Alarm," Cor grunted and pointed to the sign on the door:
EMERGENCY EXIT ONLY
ALARM WILL SOUND

Cor peeked back down the hall. He caught just enough of a glimpse to see that Tolliver disregarded Caitlyn's distraction and was heading right toward them. Caitlyn took off running down a side hallway.

"We gotta go," he wheezed.

Taylor re-adjusted the weight. He grunted, shifted and began moving across the cafeteria toward the kitchen. They passed the cash register and buffet lines and burst through the swinging kitchen doors as the bell rang. Taylor dropped to his knees and lost his hold on Cor. Both boys went down hard and sprawled across the floor.

Through the swinging doors Cor looked back to see Tolliver standing at the entrance of the lunchroom. Taylor pointed to the back of the kitchen and scurried across the kitchen floor on his hands and knees toward the loading dock. The kitchen had no windows and Cor could feel some of his energy return. He crawled along behind Taylor.

Cooks and kitchen staff stopped cooking, frying, cutting and boiling, preferring to gawk at the two freak kids crawling through their workspace.

They made it to the back door next to the loading dock and got back to their feet. Taylor burst through the door and out onto a small landing at the top of five concrete steps. A blast of direct sunlight hit Cor square in the face, instantly sapping his energy. His momentum took him through the doorway and he spilled onto the stairs outside the door. He slammed into Taylor, bounced off him and tumbled down the handful of concrete steps onto the pavement of the parking lot. The sunlight blinded him as he lay on his back. Taylor made a desperate grab at the handrail and latched on with one hand, saving himself from a nasty fall.

"Woah! Cor!" Mr. Gifford said from the shadows of an alcove next to the stairs.

Taylor hustled down the stairs and grabbed Cor's arm to hoist him up.

"Taylor, what's going on?" Mr. Gifford asked.

"Oh shoot. Mr. Gifford." Taylor hadn't known that Mr. Gifford was there. Cor's vision returned to him and he saw Mr. Gifford smoking a cigarette in the alcove.

"Is everything alright?" Gifford asked as Taylor pulled Cor off the ground. Cor grunted from the pain.

"Um yeah, Cor doesn't feel well so Caitlyn and I are taking him home. Her dad said it was okay," Taylor said unconvincingly.

"You don't have to explain anything to me. Hell, you kids are smarter than most of the teachers here." Gifford smoked his cigarette, strangely calm under the circumstances.

Caitlyn came running around the corner at the far end of the building. Taylor threw Cor's arm over his shoulders and started moving toward her powder blue VW Bug across the parking lot. He didn't see the bright blue, jacked up pickup truck with the dented passenger side door until Caitlyn slowed to a walk as she approached it. Her eyes flicked toward Taylor and Cor. The two boys instantly reversed direction back toward the stairs by the loading dock. Trace hopped out of the truck, ruining any chance Cor had of escaping with Caitlyn.

Cor and Taylor ducked behind the concrete steps.

"I thought you were going home?" Mr. Gifford said, leaning against the brick wall, finishing up his cigarette.

"Car trouble," Cor replied with a nod toward Trace. He peeked around the steps and saw Trace fully engaged in a one-sided conversation with Caitlyn. Trace then escorted her to his truck and put her in the cab before getting in after her.

"Ah," Mr. Gifford said and stubbed out his cigarette. He put the butt in his pocket, "I'll give you a ride. Wait here."

35

"What's wrong?" Mr. Gifford asked. He was behind the wheel of his van as it rumbled out of the school parking lot. "I'm sure Mrs. Baptiste could handle it."

"He has Congenital Erythropoietic Porphyria. Nothing the nurse can do for him." Taylor told Mr. Gifford. Cor was laying down on the bench seat and Taylor was up front with Mr. Gifford.

"Wow," Mr. Gifford whistled through his teeth, "sounds bad. Is it contagious?"

"Kind of, but not really," Taylor said, unable to actually lie to an authority figure. "It's an allergic reaction to the sun."

"Really? That doesn't sound like fun."

"Oh, it's not Mr. Gifford. During the day he's a mess."

A police car screamed by. It was heading toward the school with lights flashing and siren blaring. Mr. Gifford reached into the center console and dug around a bit.

"Here, try this," he said and tossed a tube of cream back at Cor.

"What is it?" Cor asked. He was already feeling better since getting in the van.

"Sunblock."

"Oh, that won't work against CEP," Taylor informed him.

"Just try it," Mr. Gifford insisted.

Cor squeezed some on his palm and rubbed it into his face and hands to humor his teacher. Another police car flew past.

"There's a lot of police around. Something must be going on. I wonder if they caught Brock's killer?" Gifford said, then changed the subject, "Cor, about your project with Caitlyn..."

"Um, Mr. Gifford," Taylor interrupted him, "no offense but I think Cor might have bigger things to worry about right now."

"Oh, okay, well I was just going to say that sometimes, it might not be a good idea to let people know that something they thought was fake is actually real. That might open a box you can't close. Do you really want people to know that vampires exist?" He said looking at Cor in the rearview mirror.

"Oh!" Taylor choked, "No! Haha!" He forced some laughter, "of course vampires don't exist. Haha! That's ridiculous."

Feeling better, Cor sat up.

"Stay down," Mr. Gifford commanded just as a police cruiser whizzed by. "You need to rest."

"Um, Mr. Gifford, this is it. This is his house." Taylor said but Mr. Gifford cruised right by without slowing down. "Mr. Gifford, you just passed it."

"Yeah, I know. I figured I'd drop you guys off around the side so you could go in the back door. You probably don't want to use the front door for a while. Right?" He turned the van down he next side street and pulled up along the curb. Taylor immediately hopped out and closed the door. Before Cor could grab the door handle Gifford turned to him.

"Cor, I know what you and Taylor are up to tonight. I heard you talking earlier. I can help. I know about the underground," he said. After the information bombs that had been dropped on Cor in the past 24 hours, this barely fazed him.

"I don't know what you're talking about."

"Yes you do Cor. I can help."

Cor slid open the door and hopped out. "No, I don't. Thanks for the ride. See you tomorrow."

"Wait..." Mr. Gifford called out but Cor had already slammed the door and slid through the neighbor's bushes. Right now, Cor didn't have time to wait.

36

Cor and Taylor snuck through the neighbor's yard and crawled through the bushes on the border between the yards. The boys stayed low to the backdoor of Cor's house. He opened the door a crack and they squeezed inside.

The windows in the house were all covered with blinds, shades, curtains or any combination of the three. If someone moved around inside, an observer would never know it from the outside. As soon as the door closed behind them Cor and Taylor were able to move around normally inside the house.

Cor crossed the kitchen and dropped his backpack on the kitchen table. He continued through into the living room. At the bay window next to the front door he peeked through the gap between the shade and the windowsill. An unmarked police car was parked at the curb across the street. Two plainclothes detectives sat in the front seats attempting to look inconspicuous, attempting to be invisible. They weren't very good at it.

Cor headed back to the kitchen and grabbed a blood bag from the refrigerator.

"Do you have wi-fi?" Taylor asked.

"I don't think Jane got the Internet hooked up yet." Cor lead Taylor down the hall to his bedroom.

"I can get on the police network though my phone but their mobile interface is worthless. I can see if there's an unsecured network around or I can hook up via satellite."

Cor's room was still a chaotic mess of half opened boxes.

"Grab a box and have a seat," Cor offered, sipping on the blood bag. Taylor sat on the floor and started digging into his backpack.

"I have a question. How come you don't dress all punk rock like they do in the movies? Like Lost Boys?"

"I don't want to stand out. The less people notice me the better. I just want to be normal." Cor said and sat on the bed.

"Good luck with that," Taylor said while setting up his laptop on the cardboard box in front of him.

"What the hell does that mean?" The tone of Cor's voice caught Taylor off guard.

"I uh, nothing. I mean. You're a teenager, in high school. I just want to be normal too. That would be a step up for me."

"You're a lot closer to normal than I am. I have to make a call."

"Use your cell. The land line is probably tapped already," Taylor suggested. He was thankful for the change in subject but still regretted his comment.

Cor went to the kitchen, fished his cell phone out of his backpack and dialed. The phone rang a few times on the other end before Caitlyn's voicemail answered. He disconnected without leaving a message, dropped it in his pocket and went back to the bedroom.

"What now?" Taylor asked.

"We wait. Caitlyn didn't answer her cell. She's probably safer with Trace than on her own anyway. The Creeper is hiding somewhere until dark. "

"Check this out," Taylor said waving Cor over to his laptop. "All of the police radio traffic is digital and gets transcribed by a voice-to-text program and stored on the servers at the station. It makes it easier to search later for reports and trials. It's also streamed as a data feed so that people on stakeouts don't give away their position with a blaring radio. I'm able to tap into that."

Lines of text scrolled up his screen like closed captioning on TV.

"I'm also able to get all of the APBs and Amber Alerts. Bad news and good news. Here's the first APB." He clicked the mouse and a window opened with some text and an old Los Angeles school photo of Cor. "Here's the good news." He clicked the mouse again and another window opened with some text and a police forensics sketch.

"That's him. That's The Creeper," Cor said. The police sketch was a drawing of the man that Cor had seen at the diner his first night in town. The man was unidentifiable in the image. Wearing dark glasses, a hat and beard his lips and nose were the only definable features. It could be anyone.

"Come on though, that could be just about anyone. Mr. Gifford, Principal Dupris? What the hell, put a fake beard and glasses on Taylor and you're a suspect. Any info on him? Address? Name? Anything?" Cor asked.

"Nothing, just that he's a person of interest and that he's been seen in the area of Odel Park."

"I guess it's a start. At least he's on their radar. Want something to drink?

"Sure."

Cor left Taylor in the bedroom to enjoy the scrolling text of the police department.

37

"Cor?" His mother said from behind him. He took a can of soda from the refrigerator, closed the door and turned to face her.

"Are you in trouble? The police were here."

"No mom, I'm fine."

"Why were the police here?"

"Probably a misunderstanding. Just go back to bed. Everything is fine." Cor tried to brush past her but Jane held out her arm to block his path to the hall.

"The police are parked out front right now. They don't do that when everything is fine. Now tell me the truth."

"You want the truth?" Cor asked, knowing that she really wanted anything but the truth. "The truth is, there's a murderer out there. The truth is, he kills just about everyone that I come in contact with. The truth is I'm the number one suspect. And the last bit of truth, the one that you refuse to believe, is that I'm a vampire! So that's the truth, and everything is fine."

"Cor, don't start this crap again. You're not a vampire. That's ridiculous. And you have nothing to do with those murders. Do you want attention? Is that what you want? Maybe we should start therapy again?"

"Open your eyes Jane! Why are you in such denial?"

"Don't talk to me like that. If your father hadn't left us…"

"Stop lying!" Cor screamed back, cutting her off. He reached over the table and grabbed his backpack. "I found this." He pulled the birth certificate out of his bag and shoved it in her face.

She took a step back and put her hands to her mouth like she had been slapped. Tears welled up in her eyes.

"Where did you get that? Were you digging around in my stuff?"

"This is MY stuff," Cor said. He had Jane on the defensive and didn't back down.

"You were never supposed to see that," she said meekly.

"Name of father," Cor read from the document, "Blakely Griffin. Seattle. And it's signed. He signed it. He was there when I was born? We left him didn't we? You always blamed him, but it was us. It was you. Why did you take that away from me? Why couldn't I have a father?"

"Because it wasn't right."

"It wasn't right? Maybe it wasn't right for you, but what about me? Did you ever consider me?"

Jane simply hid her face behind her hands and shook her head slightly.

"And what's up with your name? *Cordell?* I thought your name was *Griffin*."

"I couldn't tell you Cor," she said from behind her hands, "I didn't want you looking for him. I thought if we had the same last name you wouldn't look for him. You wouldn't care."

"Why? Why mom? Look at me and tell me why!"

"Because it wasn't right Cor," she said wiping the tears from her face. "He wasn't right." She took a deep breath. "He was like you."

"He what?"

"I never knew. I swear. I never knew! He told me after you were born. He told me what he thought he was. He said it couldn't happen. That it was impossible. He told me. He told me what you tell me. He was like you Cor. He was like you. Is that what you wanted to hear?"

"He was a vampire?"

"No Goddamnit! He was crazy! He was crazy like you!" She grabbed his shirt to send her point home but Cor flinched and pushed back. The slight shove he gave her was too much. He was stronger than he thought. She crashed into the kitchen table and fell to the floor. Cor immediately rushed to her side.

"Mom, I'm sorry. I didn't mean..."

"Leave me alone. Get away from me," she said holding her hand to her forehead. She brushed Cor back. "Leave me alone."

He stepped back from her. Their disagreements had never gone this far. Her body vibrated with sobs.

"I'll get some ice mom."

Cor stepped around the counter into the kitchen. He dug around in some drawers and cabinets looking for hand towels or dishrags. When he found them he looked to where Jane had been. She was gone.

He heard the front door open and the screen door slam closed. When Cor looked around the corner into the living room Jane was already halfway down the walkway toward the street.

He didn't think. He reacted. He bolted through the living room and charged out the front door to the front step. The sun hit him in the face. The shock of the bright light woke him up to the realization that he just made a major mistake. Jane was at the sidewalk and turned to continue storming up the street. The two cops in the unmarked car stared directly at Cor as dumbfounded as he was, their coffee cups frozen to their lips. In that split second, with the sun half blinding his eyes, Cor realized that something was different. He wasn't weak. He was normal. The sharp blast of sun should have knocked him to the ground, and left him crawling to get back inside, but he wasn't. He felt like he did before the accident. Immediately he darted back inside the house, slammed the door behind him and bolted it shut.

"Taylor!" He called out. "We have a problem!"

38

Cor ran back to his room.

"The cops saw me."

"Yeah, they just called it in." He pointed to the text on his screen. "Backup is on the way. What do we do?"

"You stay here. This is home base. They won't know you're here, and they won't come in if they think I'm somewhere else. I'm going to draw them away. You keep tabs on the police stuff and call my cell if anything comes up."

"What are you doing?"

"I'm gonna make sure the cops know I'm not here." Cor reached into one of the moving boxes and pulled out an aluminum baseball bat. "And then I'm going after The Creeper."

"But..."

Cor was out the door and down the hall before Taylor could finish his protest. He knew what Taylor would say and he hoped it was wrong. He hoped the feeling he just had wasn't a fluke.

Cor burst out the front door and down the walkway toward the sidewalk. Again he caught the undercover cops off guard. They were halfway out of the car when they froze. Hesitated. Both of them took too much time to decide what to do.

Cor made it to the sidewalk. Somehow he still felt good. There was no sign of Jane so he took off to the left and hoped the cops would pursue in their car. He ran at a full sprint down the street. Glancing back he saw the unmarked car burn rubber pulling away from the curb. Cor knew the police could only follow him in the car, they couldn't stop him and they couldn't catch him.

He felt good running in the daylight. The sun warmed his face. For the first time in four years he ran like a normal kid. He wasn't a speed freak and he wasn't weak, shuffling and sickly. Just right, like a good, strong runner.

The Crown Vic caught up and pulled up alongside him so he broke left and hopped a short chain-link fence. He cut through the backyards of a couple houses. The cop car sped up to the next corner and swung a hard left, tires screeching, down the side street. As soon as they made the turn, Cor changed direction and cut into another yard, putting four houses between the cops and himself. He changed direction again, doubling back, cutting between the houses, and then across the street behind the police car.

They had to either throw it in reverse or pull a three-point turn. Cor didn't know which option they chose but he assumed it was the wrong one. He cut through a few more yards to put more distance between them, and slowed to a walk.

Across a half dozen backyards he caught a glimpse of the unmarked car slowly rolling down a street looking for him. He made sure the police saw him so they knew he was still moving away from his house. He broke into a run again cutting through more yards and across another street. The houses were all close together with adjoining backyards and Cor was able to find an area where he was shielded from view on all sides. He felt like he could keep running forever but he stopped in the corner of a yard where a fence met a shed. He squatted down, pulled out his cell phone and made a call.

"Hello?" Taylor answered on the other end.

"Hey, what's up?" Cor said like it was any other phone call.

"What's up?" Taylor asked, his voice sounding a little panicky. "What's up with you? Are you sick? Are you safe?"

"No, I'm okay. I feel fine."

"Really? Cause I'm freakin' out over here. You can't just take off like that, you know. You're okay?"

"Yeah, maybe it was the blood I drank. What are the cops doing?"

"They have three patrol cars cruising the area looking for you. The plain clothes guys are coming back here to stake it out, in case you come back."

"Any foot patrols?"

"None yet. The call went out that you were armed and dangerous though. They're supposed to radio in before they get out of the car."

"Let me know if that happens."

"Cor, I don't like this. You have at least two hours before sunset."

"I know. Not much of a choice though."

"Hang on, I have an idea," Taylor said.

Cor peeked his head out from his corner and saw a patrol car roll slowly down an adjacent street. He could hear Taylor clicking on his computer on the other end of the phone.

"Okay, I've got it. I did a real estate search for houses for sale in the vicinity and found one that looks empty. If you can break in without being seen you can hide out til dark."

"How do you know where I am?"

"I hacked your phone and tracked the GPS."

"You can do that?"

"I just did. I'm also able to track the patrol cars through their GPS and I just saw one cruise by you. Okay, the empty house is on the corner of Cherry Street. It's three blocks south and one block west of where you are. You're clear now if you move."

"Got it."

Cor hopped to his feet and followed Taylor's directions, which led him directly to the back door of an empty house.

39

Time passed slowly in the basement of the empty house. Occasional text messages from Taylor updated Cor on the whereabouts of the police. When the sun hung low in the sky Cor moved to the ground floor of the house and dialed Caitlyn's number.

The phone on the other end rang a few times before it was answered with silence.

"Hello?" Cor asked the silence.

"Hello asshole," Trace's voice came through the phone. "We're coming to get you," he sang into Cor's ear. In the background music and voices could be heard. It sounded like a party.

"Cops are here!" Cor heard someone shout close to the phone.

"Where's Caitlyn?" Cor asked but Trace had already disconnected. He dialed Taylor's number.

"I'm heading to the diner. He's always waited for me there, no reason to think he won't show tonight. Did Jane come home yet?"

"No, and the cops haven't picked her up yet. There's something else. There was a party at the Odel Park Athletic

Field. A memorial for Brock I think. The police just broke it up."

"I just called Caitlyn's cell and Trace answered. I think he was there and I don't think she's with him."

"There weren't any arrests and no names given over the radio. The footage from the patrol car cameras gets uploaded via wi-fi or satellite to the station servers every ten minutes. I'll check it when it gets uploaded, maybe I'll see something.

"I'm going straight to the park then."

"There aren't any patrols between you and the park. If you're fast enough you can make it, no problem."

Cor watched the sun set in the distance. "Oh, I'm fast enough."

40

The sky was still grey from the receding sun, but the park was pitch black. Cor easily climbed the wrought iron fence and dropped down into the inky darkness. He avoided the main gate because that's where he would have been expected. Slipping in and out of the shadows on and off the paths slowed him down a little bit but it didn't take long for him to reach the athletic field.

The parking lot and field were empty. Cups, bottles, cans and other trash littered the fringes of the field. Candles, some of them still lit, covered a sole picnic table. Flowers, pictures and other memorabilia were laid around the table. Police tape fluttered in the breeze.

There was no sign of Caitlyn or Trace. Cor's phone buzzed.

"Yeah?" He answered.

"I got the footage," Taylor said on the other end.

"And?"

"It's hard to say, but it looks like just as the patrol car pulls into the parking lot a girl, who may or may not be Caitlyn, is walking into the woods. Alone. Judging from her body language she isn't happy."

"And Trace?"

"Yeah, he's definitely on the footage with Chuck and Trey and some other girl. According to the time stamp, the girl that looks like Caitlyn walked into the woods about fifteen minutes ago. I would bet she's still somewhere in the park."

"Okay." Cor jammed the phone into his pocket and disappeared back into the woods of Odel Park.

41

He found her in the playground. The chains squeaked against the metal S hooks as she rocked back and forth on the swing. He watched her, spying from the darkness of the tree line. He was certain that they weren't alone. There was no movement or sound from the darkness on the other side of the playground but he could feel someone else there. He slinked out of the tree line and stood behind the trunk of a massive pine along the pathway. Caitlyn swung slowly back and forth, her toes dragged in the dirt beneath the swing.

And then she stopped. Something caught her attention. The snap of a twig or the rustle of a branch. Cor had told her it was dangerous to be alone, but Trace was out of control, he was too dangerous to be around. Now she regretted her decision to leave the party. The darkness of the woods surrounding the playground seemed to close in on her. Caitlyn looked to the sky directly above. She had a clear view and could see that it was quickly darkening.

A harsh shiver wracked her body. She blamed the chilly November air, rather than admit her growing fear to herself. In the rush to get Cor out of school she had left her coat in Mr. Gifford's classroom. The thin blouse she wore did little to keep her warm. Caitlyn folded her arms in front of her chest and began walking back toward the athletic field. It felt like the safest direction to go. The path was shorter in that direction and the woods weren't so thick. The first cold drops of rain began to fall.

Hiding behind the tree along the path had been a good move. She was coming straight toward him. He wouldn't have to chase her.

A rustle in the trees across the playground grabbed her attention. She spun to face the sound and continued walking backwards, toward the path to the athletic field. He could feel her being pulled toward him. She was drawn to him. Caitlyn continued to back away from the sound at the other side of the playground. A few more steps and she would be even with him. A few more steps and he would have her.

His hand shot out from behind the tree and wrapped around her mouth in a single smooth motion. His other arm encircled her arms and body. He pulled her off her feet and toward him. Her back was pressed against his chest and his back was against the tree. He held her tight; she struggled but was no match for him.

He whispered in her ear, "Caitlyn, it's me. Shhh."

She stopped struggling but remained tense. He could feel her fear. Her heart pounded through her ribcage under his forearm. She was terrified.

"I'm not going to hurt you. He's out there. In the trees. On the other side. I'm going to let you go now. Be quiet."

He took his hand off her mouth and spun her. They were face to face.

"Cor, what are you doing here?" She whispered.

"Shhh. Just stay close to me."

Cor pulled her tight against his chest. He felt her shiver and relax slightly. She was comfortable in his arms. He could feel her heart beating against his chest. The rain fell harder.

"Who is on the other side?" She whispered into his neck.

"Brock's killer," he breathed into her ear, "he's out there. Somewhere."

"We should go to the police."

"The police can't do anything."

"Why not?"

Being this close to her made Cor feel as though their moment last night had never ended. Her misty breath encircled them, blending and swirling with his invisible exhalation. She leaned in tighter against him. Her heartbeat invaded his chest. It calmed him, energized him, it felt like his own.

"Trust me."

Cor looked over his shoulder and strained his neck to peer across the playground to the other side. He could hardly see through the pouring rain.

"I do trust you," she said faintly, "completely."

Caitlyn's scream shattered the peace of the night as her body was ripped from Cor's arms!

The Creeper wrapped one arm around her throat. A blade flashed in his other hand. Cor reacted instantly, slamming his foot into The Creeper's groin. The force of the kick lifted him off the ground forcing him to drop Caitlyn and double over in pain. Cor spun and grabbed the baseball bat from the base of the tree.

"RUN!" Cor screamed at Caitlyn, and she did, breaking off across the playground.

Cor swung the bat and slammed it into the side of The Creeper's head. The blow sent him reeling but he didn't go down.

Cor took off running after Caitlyn, catching up to her within seconds. Without breaking stride he wrapped his free arm around her waist and hoisted her up. Her feet brushed along the ground as he carried her through Odel park as fast as he could.

As he sprinted along the trails he glanced to his left. Through the pouring rain he saw The Creeper darting through the trees keeping pace with him. The Creeper was faster than Cor. With the added weight of Caitlyn, he could never outrun him.

The Odel Park main gate was just ahead of Cor and Caitlyn. The Creeper changed direction and ran straight toward them. Cor slowed his pace to let Caitlyn's feet start carrying her. The Creeper was upon them as Cor leapt into the air, spun and hurled the bat with all of his force. The business end of the bat nailed The Creeper in the throat and sent him sprawling.

Caitlyn burst out of the park at full speed. Cor was right behind her. They ran into the street, directly into the path of a pair of on-coming headlights.

The brakes locked and tires slid across the wet pavement. Cor grabbed Caitlyn to protect her but the truck stopped just before impact.

"Son of a bitch!" Trace said as he hopped out of the driver's seat. Trace's buddy Number 78 got out of the passenger seat and another one, Number 54, jumped out of the bed of the truck.

Cor released his grip on Caitlyn but she quickly grabbed his hand.

"Are you serious? This geek is here two days and you're already fucking him? I knew you were a slut." Trace said, slurring his words.

Cor turned with Caitlyn to begin walking away. Immediately a mountain slammed into his back, driving him face first into the pavement. The mountain grew arms and lifted him up. Cor's arms were pinned to his side by Number 78 in a bear hug from behind. He spun Cor so they were facing Trace and Number 54.

Trace immediately drilled Cor with a quick punch to the face. Caitlyn charged Trace but the other guy grabbed her before she made it to him.

"Trace, let's deal with this later," Cor said. Trace answered by driving his other fist into Cor's jaw.

"Trace stop!" Caitlyn pleaded. He responded with another punch.

"Trace, you don't know what you're doing," Cor said.

"Leave him alone," Caitlyn cried.

Trace grabbed her face by the jaw, while Number 54 held her.

"He killed Brock and you want me to leave him alone? Everybody knows he did it!" He dropped her face and walked back to the cab of his truck. He returned carrying a revolver.

"An eye for a fucking eye," he growled and jammed the gun in Cor's face. A flash of lightning filled the sky, followed by a burst of thunder.

"Trace!" Caitlyn cried.

"But first I'm going to make you watch me take care of my girl. Hell, I put in the time, I'm due the reward. And look, she's all wet for me."

"Trace, you're making a big mistake, just let us go."

"You made the big mistake, douche bag," he said and stuffed the gun in the back of his waistband. He grabbed Caitlyn and pushed her up against the side of the truck. Trace wrapped his hand around her throat and held her head still. He forced his lips against hers. Caitlyn struggled against him, flailing her arms. His hand tightened around her throat and pushed her harder against the truck. His other hand flashed by and slapped her face.

Cor struggled to break free from the grip of the beast holding him. He couldn't get any leverage to build up force against the three-hundred pounder restraining him.

Trace thrust his free hand up Caitlyn's wet blouse. She flailed back at him. He retaliated with another, harder smack that knocked the fight out of her.

"Trace, don't do this," Cor urged, shouting over the pounding rain.

"Keep that piece of shit under control," Trace ordered his meatheads. He wrapped his arms under Caitlyn and dragged her to the back of the truck. He lifted her up, dropped her in the bed and climbed in after her.

Cor tilted his head back and felt it press against Number 78's cheek.

Perfect.

He thrust his head forward and slammed it back. The back of his head smashed into Number 78's nose. The mountain dropped his hold on Cor and stumbled back. He reached up clutching at his nose, which had exploded all over his face. Cor spun and cocked his arm back to put him out but the other meathead grabbed a hold of him and wrapped him up in a half—nelson. Number 78 saw his chance and took it. He drilled Cor in the face with his massive knuckles, the lunchbox sized fist slammed into Cor's cheek. Cor thrust his foot into Number 78's knee. His leg bent in an unnatural direction. Big Number 78 dropped to the ground howling, his football career over.

Cor grabbed the other meathead's arm and flipped him over with a hip toss. Number 54 rolled with it and popped back up to his feet. He took one step toward Cor but Cor's fist found a home in the center of his meaty face before his second foot hit the ground. Cor felt Number 54's nose give way under the force of the blow. He crumpled to the ground. Down and out.

"What the hell is going on?" Trace popped his head up from the bed of the truck. Cor turned his attention toward the last man standing.

"Get away from her," Cor demanded. Trace stood in the back of the truck. As soon as Cor got within range Trace punted him in the jaw. The force of the kick spun Cor and dropped him to his knees. The quarterback jumped out of the truck and drove his fist into his enemy's face. He attempted to follow that with an uppercut but Cor grabbed Trace's fist out of midair air.

Cor got to his feet. He controlled Trace with his grip on the quarterback's fist. Trace's knuckles and bones begin to bend in Cor's hand.

"No! No! Not my right! Not my right!" Trace screamed.

Cor squeezed harder and felt the bones snap, knuckles pop and tendons tear. Trace dropped to his knees. Tears streamed down his face mixing with the pouring rain. Cor grabbed the football star by the back of the head and drove his face into the side of the truck. Trace fell to the ground, twisted, his throwing days a thing of the past.

Cor made his way to the back of the truck. Caitlyn was gathering herself and buttoning her blouse.

"Are you okay?" Cor asked, offering his hand.

"Yeah, he hits like a girl," she said with a sniffle.

"You're dead, fucker."

Cor turned just in time to see the barrel of Trace's gun flash. The gunshot knocked him to the ground. His stomach filled with pain. Cor clutched at his gut and rolled over to his hands and knees. Caitlyn's screams were drowned out by a burst of thunder. Cor spit a mouthful of blood into the rainwater river flowing down the street. He felt the steel of the barrel pressed against his scalp.

"Self defense," Trace said, "I'll be a hero."

Cor's fist flew straight upward catching Trace clean under his chin. The blow sent him flying back. He landed flat on his back, his arms and legs stiff and his jaw jutting out the side of his face.

"You have to get out of here," Cor said to Caitlyn, the pain in his stomach receding. She stared back at him in shock. "My house is three blocks up and two blocks to the left. Number forty two Drury Street. Taylor is there. Do not call the cops. The back door is unlocked. Go in the back."

She stared at him. "He shot you," she said quietly.

"He missed. Did you hear me?"

"Huh? Yeah." She snapped out of it.

"Go to my house. No cops. Taylor is there. Got it?"

"Where are you going?"

"Just go."

Cor turned toward Odel Park but stopped when he felt the gentle weight of her hand on his forearm. She turned him toward her. Now he was the one drawn to her. Caitlyn's hand rose and landed lightly on his wet cheek. She easily pulled him in. He couldn't resist.

Her lips connected with his. Their breath combined. Their souls merged. Her heart pounded in his head. He corrupted her purity. The kiss lasted an eternity and ended too soon. Cor pulled away, before he damaged her forever.

"You have to go. I'll be there soon," Cor released her hand and disappeared into the park.

Caitlyn picked up Trace's revolver from the flooding street.

42

Cor was a few feet into the opaque darkness of Odel Park when his phone buzzed. The caller ID read *JANE*.

He answered it, "Mom?"

"Cor?" Jane's strained voice came through from the other end. Her voice was quickly replaced with a man's rough bark that Cor didn't recognize.

"You have twenty minutes to kill the girl and turn yourself in to the police or I kill your mother." The call dropped.

Cor picked up the pace moving through the park and dialed Taylor's number.

"Hey," Taylor answered.

"The Creeper has my mother. He just called me on her phone. He told me to kill Caitlyn and turn myself in or he'll kill Jane."

"Shit."

"I found Caitlyn but ran into trouble with Trace and his friends."

"Bad?"

"Yeah, the football team won't have a winning season this year. The good news is that bullets don't kill me." Cor ran his hand over the bloody hole in his hoodie. "I'm looking for The

Creeper now. He's gotta have her in the park. That's where everything keeps happening."

"You said he called on her cell?"

"Yeah."

"If I can get a call through I can hack the GPS, like I did with yours."

"I doubt he'll answer a call from you though."

"Yeah, but he'll answer one from you. We'll call him back and tell him you did it. I'll set up a conference call and I can sink the hack that way. Hang on."

Cor heard a digital click. The screen lit up and automatically scrolled through to RECENT CALLS. The listing from Jane's call lit up and the phone dialed. After one ring the call was answered with silence.

"Hello?" Cor said.

"Did you do it?" The man's voice asked.

"Yes, she's dead. I'm waiting for the police to arrive. Put my mother on."

"Where?"

"By the swing set."

"You better hope they show quick. You only have twelve minutes left."

"I did what you said, now put Jane on!" Cor commanded.

"Cor?" Jane's voice came over the phone.

"Eleven minutes," The Creeper said and the call disconnected. Cor's phone buzzed again and he answered.

"Did you get that?" He asked Taylor.

"Yeah, I have to hack it now and turn on her GPS. Might take a few minutes."

"You have less than ten. I'll keep looking. I told Caitlyn to go to my house. She should be there in a few."

43

Cor headed straight to the swing set where he found Caitlyn earlier. He hoped that The Creeper might show up to get an eyewitness confirmation that he had killed Caitlyn. He was drawn to the tree where he and Caitlyn had hidden earlier. He could feel her as though her body was still pressed to his. He felt her mist still swirling around the tree in the rain. His cell phone buzzed interrupting his reverie.

"The phone is under an old stone bridge about 1,000 feet to the west of where you are." Taylor said exasperated.

"I'm going there now," Cor said about to hang up the phone.

"Wait! Caitlyn hasn't shown up yet," Taylor shouted before Cor disconnected.

Cor felt the disturbance and instinctively ducked before he knew why.

The fire axe sliced through the air just above his head and was buried into the tree next to him.

Cor's cell phone flew from his hand. He spun and was face to face with The Creeper. Cor thrust his foot into The Creeper's midsection sending the older man flying back, crashing into the swing set. Cor grabbed the handle of the axe and tried to pull it from the tree. The blade of the axe was buried deep and wouldn't budge.

The Creeper recovered from the kick and charged at Cor. As he collided with the boy, the impact helped Cor pull the axe free from the tree. The two of them slammed into the mud and scrambled to their feet. Cor managed a lackluster swing. The Creeper dodged it easily and retaliated with a straight right fist to Cor's eye. The hard blow spun him. He used the momentum to swing the axe around again, slamming the flat of the blade against the side of The Creeper's head.

The Creeper stumbled into the swings. Cor followed up right behind. He swung the axe wildly, clanging it off the steel piping of the swing set. He swung again backing The Creeper up as it rattled off the chains. The Creeper stumbled between the pipes and chains still dazed. He lost his footing and fell backward onto his back. Cor hoisted the axe over his head and brought it down hard to split The Creeper's face in two.

The Creeper's hands clapped together stopping the blade in midair, mere centimeters from cleaving his face. Cor bore down harder on the handle of the axe burying it deep into the ground as The Creeper slipped to the side. Before Cor could recover The Creeper was on his feet and drove a kick into the younger man's face.

The kick knocked Cor flat on his back, dazed. The Creeper yanked the axe from the ground and swung it, smashing the side of Cor's face with the flat of the blade. The blow brought Cor close to unconsciousness. He was unable to move as The Creeper stood over him.

Without warning The Creeper's chest exploded. The crack of a gunshot filled the air. Two more shots immediately followed.

Caitlyn stood at the edge of the playground, Trace's smoking gun in her hand. The Creeper dropped to his knees and slumped to the ground.

She ran to Cor who still lay on the ground, his thoughts scrambled from the blow he took.

"Cor, get up. Please, get up."

"What's going on? What's happening!" Taylor's disembodied voice emitted from Cor's cell phone somewhere in the mud.

The Creeper groaned and sat up.

Caitlyn pulled Cor tighter to her body. "Stay away from him!" She screamed.

The Creeper pulled his feet under him and stood. Caitlyn raised the gun and fired point blank. The shot exploded into The Creeper's chest. He stumbled slightly from the impact, stepped forward and backhanded her into unconsciousness.

44

The Creeper bound Cor's wrists behind his back using a heavy gauge wire. Then he tied up Caitlyn and hoisted her over his shoulder. He grabbed Cor's hood and dragged him through the woods. A thousand feet to the west, they ended up in a dried creek bed under an old rock bridge, The Creeper's home base, just as Taylor had said.

Jane was hanging from the bridge, suspended by ropes around her wrists. The Creeper dragged Cor over to the base of the bridge and left him leaning against the rocks. He dropped Caitlyn on the ground next to Cor.

A beam of moonlight struck The Creeper across the face as he stood. For the first time Cor saw him without his hat. For the first time Cor saw him without his glasses. For the first time, Cor recognized him.

45

The L.A. summer sun was hot and bright. Cor's shirt was soaked with sweat but it didn't matter. It had been a good game and Cor was the hero. He ran to his mother's car, the bag of gear slung over his shoulder banging against his leg. His left leg was scuffed with dirt all the way up from his shin to his shirt. It was a welcome side effect from his game-winning slide into home.

Jane was waiting for him on the edge of the parking lot closest to the dugout. He got to the car, chucked his bag into the back seat and was about to hop in the front seat when his mother stopped him.

"Uh uh," she said wagging her finger, "brush off first."

He did a quick pat down and kicked some dirt off his cleats. He never understood what she was so worried about, the car was a piece of junk.

She was on break and only had enough time to pick Cor up from the game and drop him off at home before she had to be back at the hospital.

He hopped into the front seat, shut his door and they were on their way. Jane pulled out of the parking lot as Cor tried to buckle up. The seatbelt always had problems. Most of the time it locked up before it could be extended far enough to be fastened. Cor kept tugging and releasing, attempting to get the self-locking mechanism to loosen. The seatbelt wouldn't move more than a few inches.

"Another shutout?" Jane asked as they cruised down the street.

"Nah, they're in second place so they're pretty good," he replied, still tugging at the seatbelt. "They got a few runs off of me but we beat 'em. I nailed an in-the-park homer in the ninth."

"I bet everybody loved that," she said with a grin.

"Yeah, I got the game ball again." Cor tugged at the seatbelt some more. "Mom, what the heck is wrong with this stupid seatbelt?"

Cor took his eyes off the seatbelt for a moment and looked out the windshield. Jane's compact car cruised into the intersection at the same time as a minivan from the cross street. The van was directly in front of them. There was no time to react.

The bumper of her car slammed into the side door of the minivan throwing Cor forward. He lifted from his seat. His face made contact with the windshield and then burst through the safety glass. He passed through the short space over the hood of the car as the front end disappeared, slicing into the side of the van. As he passed through the air, Cor saw a small child in a car seat strapped to the middle bench seat of the van. The bumper of his mother's car continued to press forward, closer and closer to the child. Cor's face struck the roof of the van and he lost sight of the child, the bumper and their impending meeting. The impact spun Cor through the air, flipping him over the roof of the van. He landed face first on the pavement and slid.

He lay on the hot pavement watching the two vehicles twist and smoke and shatter. A small pond of his blood grew around him on the asphalt. As his body drained, he lost consciousness.

Days later Cor was comatose in his hospital bed, only aware of the world around him as though it were a dream. The machines surrounding him beeped and blipped. People outside his room were talking. Cor couldn't clearly hear what they were saying but he had heard the words *brain damage* and *No chance of recovery*. He thought they were talking about him. He felt brain damaged. He was in a fog, unable to respond and react. The voices outside the door grew louder. Angrier.

The door burst open and a man, a crazed man, barged into the room. A nurse attempted to stop the man but he shoved her violently against the wall. The crazed man charged Cor's hospital bed and lunged across it. Cor couldn't move. He was powerless to react. He lay there as the crazed man clamped his hands around his throat. The man was screaming and spitting and foaming with rage.

"Your mother trapped my boy!" He screamed, "I'll kill you!"

With the crazed man's hands closing his throat, Cor's body reacted, moved instinctively. His mouth opened wide and his head thrust forward. Cor's teeth latched down on the crazed man's forearm. The man howled and retreated as though his arm were ablaze. Blood flowed between the fingers wrapped around the bite. The crazed man fled from the room. Cor never saw him again.

46

That crazed man now stood before Cor.

"What do you want? Why are you doing this?" Jane cried.

"Your son knows," The Creeper said.

"The accident, mom. He was the other driver," Cor explained.

"Accident?" The Creeper spit. "Accident? That was no accident! My son! My baby boy! He wasn't turned into a vegetable by accident!" The Creeper screamed, flying into a rage.

"I'm sorry!" Jane cried back.

"You're sorry? You're sorry?" The Creeper got in her face, "you took my son from me! Sorry doesn't work! And this monster..." He drove his foot into Cor's midsection sending him hard into the mud. "Bites me! Poisons me! Forces me to kill for food. For blood! Every murder is on his hands! He will live in a cell forever! A life sentence for every murder. And you," he turned to Jane, "will watch him, trapped inside that prison for the rest of your life, the same way that I watch my son trapped in the prison of his body."

Caitlyn stirred, beginning to return to consciousness.

"One last murder," The Creeper snarled at Cor.

"HELP!!" Jane called out hoping someone could hear above the pounding rain and thunder. The Creeper silenced her with a quick punch that knocked her out. He turned back toward Caitlyn and hoisted her up like a doll. She was still stunned. The Creeper snapped open his knife and put the blade to her neck.

"Her blood is on your hands," he sneered at Cor. The tip of the blade disappeared into her flesh.

A loud KLANG filled the air when the aluminum bat slammed into the back of The Creeper's head. Taylor's blow was enough to knock The Creeper's head sideways. The attack surprised him and he dropped Caitlyn and the knife into the mud.

Taylor wound up to swing again. He brought the bat down as hard as he could on The Creeper's back. The strike barely fazed him.

The Creeper grabbed the bat with one hand and ripped it from Taylor's grasp. His other hand shot out and latched onto Taylor's throat. The Creeper tossed the bat to the ground and lifted Taylor into the air by the neck.

"Even better," he growled.

Cor strained against the wires binding his wrists. The steel lines cut into his flesh.

Taylor clawed and scratched at The Creeper's hand choking off his breath.

A man charged from out of the darkness slamming into The Creeper. The new attacker tackled him from behind, smashing him violently into the muddy ground and freeing Taylor.

The Creeper and his attacker rolled through the mud and separated. They both sprang to their feet and squared off. The attacker's hood fell away and Mr. Gifford stood face to face with The Creeper.

The wire cut deeper into Cor's wrists as he strained against them.

"Mr. Gifford! Run! He's a..." Cor couldn't finish his warning. The Creeper threw three lightning fast punches. Mr. Gifford moved just as fast. He dodged the first two and blocked the third. The teacher then retaliated with a flurry of punches and kicks of his own.

The two men were equally matched going blow for blow with amazing speed. Punches, blocks and kicks all happened in a blur. Mr. Gifford threw a roundhouse kick that missed but backed his adversary up enough to allow Mr. Gifford to dive for the axe.

He popped up to his feet wielding the weapon. Spinning, whirling and swinging the axe like a tornado, he backed The Creeper up against the rock bridge. Gifford had a clear shot and swung the axe, burying it deep into the stone. The Creeper managed to avoid the blow and reached for the baseball bat. In a single move he grabbed the bat and cracked Mr. Gifford in the back of the head.

Mr. Gifford maintained his hold on the axe as the hit knocked him to the ground. Using the axe he blocked The Creeper's next attack. The bat was raised again. Mr. Gifford swung the axe, knocking The Creeper's legs out from under him. Mr. Gifford sprang to his feet and brought the axe down on The Creeper. He got the bat up at the last second deflecting the teacher's blow. The attack chopped off the end of the bat leaving a sharp, jagged edge.

Mr. Gifford lost his balance from the missed swing and stumbled forward. The Creeper thrust the bat at Mr. Gifford, plunging the sharpened end into his chest! The Creeper got to his feet with Mr. Gifford impaled on the bat. The Creeper shoved the teacher against the tree, passing the bat through him and into the trunk. He had pinned Mr. Gifford to the tree like a thumbtack to a bulletin board.

Cor felt the wire hit the bone and flexed with all of his strength. With no more flesh to slice through the wire snapped! He grabbed The Creeper's knife from the mud and jumped into the air. He easily crossed the twenty feet to The Creeper in a single bound.

Cor landed on him, driving his feet into the other man's chest and smashing him to the ground. Cor dropped to his knees and mounted him, sitting on The Creeper's chest. He went berserk with the knife! Slicing! Jabbing! Cutting!

Bone-deep gashes opened up across The Creeper's face. Blood sprayed through the air like a sprinkler. The knife gouged deep into The Creeper's eye. He raised a hand to defend himself but the knife stabbed easily through his palm. With a second swipe The Creeper lost two fingers. He desperately threw his other hand up and knocked the bloody knife from Cor's grasp.

Cor continued the assault, pummeling him with his fists. He could feel The Creeper's skull crack and crumble as his hands rained down on it.

Cor lunged forward and thrust his mouth onto The Creeper's neck. He latched his teeth deep into the flesh. Cor's mouth filled with The Creeper's blood. The Creeper slipped a leg in under Cor and shoved him off, sending him through the air. Cor landed at Mr. Gifford's feet and spit a chunk of The Creeper's neck into the mud.

The Creeper pulled himself to his feet. Blood poured from his wounds. It flowed out in crimson rivers, mixing with the pouring rain. Half blind and crippled he knew he was defeated and turned to retreat. Cor grabbed the axe and charged.

He buried the axe deep into The Creeper's back. The mortally wounded man dropped to his knees. Cor yanked it free and struck again sending The Creeper face down into the mud. He brought the axe down again and again. The Creeper clawed at the mud in a vain attempt to pull himself away like a worm. Another swipe of the axe snapped the handle as the head chopped into The Creeper's back. Chunks of flesh were separated from his back, whole sections of his ribcage were gone, yet his fingers still pulled at the mud.

Through the gaping holes in The Creeper's back Cor could see his enemy's black, poisoned heart, barely beating. He plunged the lower half of the broken axe handle through The Creeper's back sending the wooden spike straight through the heart. The makeshift stake paralyzed him instantly, pinning him to the ground. The Creeper's fingers and limbs stiffened. With his final blow Cor brought the blade of the axe down on The Creeper's neck, severing his head in one fell swoop.

His foe dispatched, Cor turned his attention back to his friends.

Taylor kneeled over Caitlyn, his hand wrapped tightly around her throat. Blood oozed through his fingers and mixed with the mud that she lay in.

"It doesn't look good," Taylor said.

Cor dropped to his knees beside her and cradled her head. He could feel the strength of her soul quickly fading. Her breath was shallow, no longer strong enough to swirl in misty clouds around him. Her heartbeat no longer resounded through him.

"I'm sorry," he whispered to her.

"Save me," she breathed back.

"I can't," Cor said, more to himself than to her.

"Cor, I think you can," Taylor said to him.

"No Taylor, it's a curse."

"Save me." Caitlyn struggled with the words. She wrapped her delicate hand around the back of Cor's neck and pulled him forward until their mouths met. Through the kiss he felt the last of her pure white soul escape her body.

He pulled back from her lips and released a primal howl into the pouring rain. Hellfire pain ripped through his mouth. His canine teeth eased forth, growing out of his gums with a rush of blood and ripping pink flesh.

Cor felt the final throb of Caitlyn's heart. He lunged forward and thrust his fangs deep into the flesh of her neck. Every muscle tensed and spasmed as his poison flowed into her bloodstream and altered her.

He pulled back from her throat. Convulsions wracked her body. The poison assaulted her very being and every cell battled back against the change. What little blood she had left flowed from the knife wound in her neck and oozed from her eyes, nose and ears, expelled by the new fluids coursing through her veins. The wound slowly began to knit together, leaving a thick scar as her human tissue mingled with the new flesh. Cor cradled her writhing body in his arms, her heartbeat barely fluttered, the mist from her exhalation gone. He had saved her.

Taylor made his way to the grotesque sight of Mr. Gifford pinned to the tree by the aluminum baseball bat.

"Oh man, Mr. Gifford," Taylor said. Mr. Gifford's eyes flicked open sending a shock through the young genius. "Holy shit!"

"Jesus, this hurts. Good thing it isn't hard rock Canadian maple though."

"Oh my God!" Taylor exclaimed.

Mr. Gifford grabbed the bat with both hands and slowly pulled it out of the tree. He dropped to his knees as he became unstuck and pulled the bat out the rest of the way. Taylor ducked behind a tree and vomited.

Mr. Gifford paused for a moment, allowing himself some time to recover before getting to his feet. He made his way to the bridge and went directly to Cor's mother. He lifted her up, freeing her bound hands from where they were secured to the bridge. As he set her carefully on the ground her eyes opened. She regained consciousness. Her eyes grew wide when she saw Mr. Gifford's face.

"Blake?" She asked with shock in her voice.

The name registered in Cor's head. It sounded familiar, and then he placed it.

"Blake? Blakely? Blakely Griffin?" Cor said in disbelief.

"Hello son.

47

"In conclusion, humans primarily create myths using personal information and experiences," Caitlyn told the class.

"Many pieces of art reveal myths throughout history. Sometimes these pieces were based on reality." Cor continued. He was standing beside Caitlyn in front of their Art History class. "For example, the work we have shown you here today."

"From these examples we can determine that there is a good possibility that unicorns and pterippi have actually existed in the past and could still exist today." Caitlyn concluded their presentation and waved her arm out like a game show hostess over numerous paintings and drawings of winged and horned horses. The finale of their presentation drew some sighs, eye rolling and light, sarcastic applause from their classmates.

"Tomorrow Diana and Wes will be presenting," Mr. Gifford said just before the school bell interrupted him. "Nice work kids, I think the class enjoyed it."

"Sure they did," Caitlyn said while packing up the art and materials from the presentation.

Cor slung his backpack over his shoulder and grabbed Caitlyn's books. She took his free hand in hers.

"Hey," Mr. Gifford handed Caitlyn a tube of cream, "It's pretty bright out there today."

"Thanks," Cor said.

The young couple stepped into the hallway where Taylor was waiting among the throngs of students rushing to class.

"You gotta see the results of this autopsy," He said, his nose buried in a medical folder. He joined the two bloodsuckers as they disappeared into the crowd, just three normal teenagers.

This was only the beginning.

About the author:

Nathan Wrann is a writer, publisher and independent filmmaker living in Connecticut with his rescued Chihuahua, Napoleon; pain-in-the-ass cat, Konstantine and wife Kimberly. His films, HUNTING SEASON, and BURNING INSIDE are currently available on DVD and VOD.

Made in the USA
Charleston, SC
04 February 2012